JULIA DREAM

Fabia Scali-Warner

Julia Dream

Julia Dream

ISBN 978-1-48359-505-4

www.viralstorytelling.com

Julia Dream

*To the hypocrisy of petty bureaucrats, corrupt justice,
and superficial judges that have allowed me
to distill the hate I need
to write what I write;*

*...but also to all the people I love,
that in reading me complete my redemption.*

Julia Dream

I

The clouds were rolling, distant and undisturbed, and a veiled sky reflected in her gaze, metallic and gray as a stormy sea. Moisture stagnated in the air, drawn by a wind that seemingly cut off all chances of rain.

Julia's eyes followed the grayness of the sky and its blinding glare on the marble columns of the Ministry, worn and polished by time. The building was very old, surely older than the First Cataclysm. After all, Cleo often observed that the European shield had revealed itself one of the strongest.

She tensed the muscles of her back, trying to remove the uniform clinging to her shoulder blades, sticky with sweat. It had been a calm day, without duels, but the heat and the low gray sky were overwhelming.

"Nice welcome our capital is giving the Emperor" she whispered to herself.

The Capital and the Itinerant Court were transferring that very day to Province I, Julia's province. That was one of the reasons why the day had been so calm. Most of the soldiers and generals usually buzzing around the

Julia Dream

Ministry, seeking more weapons and resources for their regiments, were now attending the solemn parade in front of the Emperor of the Earth, who was returning from a long institutional trip in distant galaxies.

The identification badge woven in the right sleeve of the uniform's suit shivered slightly, distracting Julia from her thoughts and reporting the end of her shift. Many employees had been granted a two-hour leave, to allow them to attend the ending of the welcoming parade and the official entry of the Emperor in the Palace.

She returned to the main body of the Ministry to recover her dinner, her salary; two liters of purified $H2O$, a white pill for sugars, a red one for protein, and a green capsule for vitamins. A full meal. The water was good, courtesy of the Cornell family: the best synthesized water of the Empire, if you listened to the gossip of the soldiers.

Julia moved with methodical gestures: she carefully placed the pills in a small transparent box, inserting it in one of the diagonal pockets of her coat, just below her breast, and quickly closing the silvery zipper. She then drank a sip from the bottle of water, placing it on the tripod that furnished her small compartment in the Ministry and immediately screwing the cap back on with care; then she fastened the scabbard of her service sword in a resting position (from her side to her shoulders), finally picking up the bottle and leaving her small room, covering the stairs and corridors of the Ministry with long, quick strides. Her pace gave away a restlessness and an agitation that were perhaps due to an unusual surplus of energies - for the first time in two years she was ending her shift after less than twelve hours of work.

She walked without rushing along the pedestrian scaffoldings of the City, always heading uphill. There was little traffic, and she actually found herself going against the tide, since many people were climbing down to watch the parade in the Maximum Square. As for her, she was counting on a view from above.

The last escalator ran close to the tall walls of the villas of the nobility, for once probably empty: the Chemical Aristocracy of the City stood at the right of the Emperor in his triumph. The science of the noble families fed and sheltered the citizens of the Empire, and the Empire recognized and honored this power.

From the highest scaffolding Julia finally turned her back to the villas, despite the fascination she felt for them, to look down on the City, dominated in the distance by the dome of the Palace and brushed in that moment by the last rays of a crimson sunset. The distant flags of the parade seemed to absorb the color, engulfed in the dusty atmosphere of the day's end. She could not distinguish clearly the crest of the Imperial Black Moon, but it was there, as it was everywhere.

It lasted a couple of minutes, then evening crept in. The lights of the buildings turned on in unison, while in the square the procession towards the Palace began with a sparkle of torches. Deciding she had seen enough, Julia took the flight of escalators towards her condominium.

✧

She lived in a fairly central residential district. Two years had passed since the fire that had killed her parents. She had been allowed to continue living with Cleo in their parents' house, since Julia had been quick to adapt to her new duties, a quality that had parachuted her in a good job in the Ministry of Counter-Terrorism. She was required to have the organizational skills necessary to manage the distribution of weapons to the different regiments of the Army, the diplomacy to deal with the generals, and the skill with the sword needed to solve controversy by dueling.

The Empire deemed that non-lethal duels to first blood were the most efficient way of solving issues between citizens - annoying to the right point, to put off an overflow of contentiousness, yet not dangerous enough to weaken the government. Furthermore, they settled things quickly. Julia was grateful that Ministry welfare included in her contract all medical expenses, wounds with internal regeneration included.

She didn't take long to reach her condominium. It was a building made of dark concrete, no different from the others in the area, well connected to the escalators that led to the city center. She looked up - the outer window on the thirteenth floor was lit, so Cleo had already returned.

The entrance door opened automatically in recognizing Julia's badge as she passed by, and she could hear the metallic noise of the elevator descending from the upper levels of the building. As she heard its arrival, Julia distractedly opened the old door, her gaze distant, trained on far-away memories. Two female figures suddenly found themselves staring at each other, as if ambushed by some common dark fear.

Julia Dream

An old lady was staring at Julia with wide eyes, as if she had seen the image of the Grim Reaper in that pale girl with black hair and a sword. At the same time Julia met that gaze - rare with its old age - with a shiver of fear, as if Death were manifesting itself to her with gray hair curled in old rollers and dusty slippers of pink sponge.

It was only a moment - then whispering apologetic words both women moved on in their opposite directions.

◈

Cleo was curled up on a sofa in front of the door. This opened with a rustle, letting Julia in. She rose to greet her sister with a quick hug and a kiss on her cheek, welcoming her with a smile. Even though she was blonde, while Julia had dark hair, Cleo's looks immediately revealed her kinship with her sister, as they shared the same profile and eyes, even if Julia's were stormy and gray and Cleo's deep and green like the Forest surrounding the city.

Julia answered her sister's welcome with a smile.

"Not at the parade, I see."

Cleo shook her head, and her curls.

"No, but I did get to visit the Palace with the class today, to study its design."

Julia's good work at the Ministry had granted a renovation of Cleo's Education Permit, and Cleo was happy when she talked of her studies, displaying rare enthusiasm.

Cleo continued her tale, anticipating the questions to come.

"The Palace is... incredible. We're used to seeing the Dome from a distance, but inside... it looks like the entrance to another world. There are statues of children with wings, and paintings of glowing men, and columns, and polished stone... The throne of the Emperor is right in the middle of a golden structure of spiraling columns..."

Julia listened to her attentively, in silence, trying to keep the fire in her sister's eyes alive.

"I wonder what all those images meant, at the time" Cleo continued, while her gaze clouded.

"A really significant part of our knowledge was lost with the Cataclysm" she sighed.

"We did leave a lot of negative stuff behind, though" Julia answered.

"Consider that women had no birth control implant, bled once a month, and grew children in their bellies."

A slight shiver betrayed the disgust she felt for this condition.

"It's actually possible that some were socially discriminated because of their biology, at least this is what I remember from my history books."

"True" Cleo nodded.

"But did you know that some aristocratic women today decide not to grow their children in the artificial uterus, and follow a so-called natural pregnancy?"

Julia theatrically arched her eyebrows at this new eccentricity. As a high-level student Cleo had more dealings with the aristocracy than she did, and would sometimes tell the tales of their habits.

"I suppose they are allowed to slacken their work performance, or have nothing better to do."

"Or they have the feeling that something was lost with the control implant, after all" Cleo added thoughtfully.

Night had completely fallen; the murmur of the escalators quivered into a sharp snap, then went off. The city was shutting down for the hours of rest.

"Counter-Terrorist Julia Mayne, report for duty."

A tired voice penetrates through the videophone, interrupts the night, sleep and regularity of life, final like the rustle of signed and stamped papers.

"Counter-Terrorist Julia Mayne, rep..."

No irritation, only fatigue in the voice interrupted by the panting answer of a disheveled girl, blandly dressed in a tank top, addressing a quick and courteous salute to the screen.

"I'm here, Supervisor. Forgive my delay."

On the other side of the monitor the Supervisor shrugged off the girl's excuses with a quick gesture of her hand, gloved in Ministerial red.

"No matter. I sent a Spider to pick you up. You have 4 minutes and 30 seconds."

Julia answered with a mechanic salute, while Supervisor Yrenes shut the communication, leaving the screen shiny, silvery, and empty.

"Julia, what's happening?"

Cleo was staring at her sister with wide eyes, sitting on the bed with her knees at her breast and a thin sheet pulled up to her chin, hiding half of her face. Julia was pulling up the trousers of her uniform and answered from the bathroom, where she had gone for a quick wash.

"I don't know."

Her tone was dark. The bright clock indicated the time was 03.22 a.m., which left her about two minutes' time before the arrival of the Spider. An uncommon event like a night call combined with the arrival of the Emperor's Itinerant Court was hard to consider a coincidence.

She closed the uniform's blazer, acknowledging the familiar vibration coming from the identification badge as it activated with the DNA of her skin. She picked up the sword from the foot of the bed, slung it over her shoulder and headed without a word to the door.

"Julia!"

Cleo's voice was frightened, like her eyes.

"Be careful."

Julia traced back her steps, lost 20 seconds to give her sister a kiss and a nervous smile.

"I will."

And she went out in the night.

⋘

Stars covered by clouds, and light years away, anyway. The stopwatch showed 23 seconds to impact, the arrival of the Spider - and indeed she saw him, a distant movement in the maze of scaffoldings and stairs, a dart just barely reflected in metal, a darker shade in the opaque night.

The figure got closer and closer, following impossible trajectories, and finally landed on its feet a few meters away from Julia.

"I'm the Imperial Messenger n.9."

Julia stepped forward, giving a closer look at the sharp features of a man of indefinite age, slender yet powerful in build; shiny black ropes ran from a central gear looking like a double backpack placed on his back and on his sternum.

She addressed him with a respectful nod of her head.

"Level II Counter-Terrorist Mayne."

The Spider nodded.

"Have you ever traveled with an Imperial Messenger?"

Julia shook her head, perhaps showing some of her anxiety.

"No problem. Hold on to me."

Julia Dream

The man said nothing else, and started attaching snap-hooks to Julia's uniform, assuring her to his equipment. She found herself almost perfectly stuck with her torso to the bundle of ropes on the Spider's chest, arms and legs suddenly helpless when the Messenger threw the first rope that took them dangling several meters in the air, hanging from the railing of Escalator 102.

"You may place your hands on my shoulders, if you wish." Then the trip began, with the wind of their bold trajectories in her hair and the clouds glimpsed under her feet, with trembling hands and a suddenly conspicuous heartbeat, accelerated by the hallucinated and dream-vivid sensation of never experimented or imagined speed. The Spider balanced weights, calculated arches and falls with extraordinary grace, softened jolts and jerks with the elastic fibers of the right cables, and allowed different perspectives of the city.

Something deeper than Julia's nerves had been shaken, when after a few minutes they touched the ground next to the imposing marble bulk of the Ministry. She thanked the Spider with inexplicably moist eyes.

He answered with a vague smile and a respectful salute that was in no way due to a lower ranking officer such as

Julia – then disappeared in the rooftops leaving behind only the faint echo of his undecipherable voice.

"Farewell, Counter-Terrorist Mayne. They're waiting for you."

❦

The squeak of her faux leather boots echoed in the silence of the hallowed marble corridors. The slightly unreal light of the emergency generators followed Julia on her route, lighting up and turning off after her passage. Long, worried steps took her to the office of the Supervisor that had summoned her - a blondish, olive-skinned woman who was looking slightly haggard in the red clothing typical of Imperial functionaries. Her darkened eyelids and ringed eyes told the tale of an abrupt wake-up call. She was waiting, sitting behind an antique wooden desk, her arms tight on her lap, fingers crossed on her belly.

"Supervisor Yrenes."

Julia limited herself to saluting from the doorstep.

"Come in, and sit down."

The girl obeyed.

"Less than an hour ago Province P has declared war on the Empire."

"What? But it's madness!"

"They want to break off and organize an independent political entity."

Julia's face, albeit controlled, betrayed from the expression of her eyes the very quick passage from perplexity to astonishment, from astonishment to concern, and from concern to fear.

"And how does this war involve us?"

Yrenes ignored the question.

"Province P has already appointed a delegate to solve this problem with a duel to the death, as dictated by tradition. One of their fencing champions, a professional athlete - they feel quite confident of their victory."

"Is the Empire really going to allow Province P to break off, should they win?"

The pause in the rhythm of the conversation was barely detectable, despite the stillness of the functionary's gaze - what was the Supervisor feeling? Fatigue? Disdain for such a naïve question?

"Of course not. Should we lose, the Imperial Army will occupy the region."

"What role do we have in this matter?"

This time Yrenes decided to answer.

"We are hosting the Itinerant Court. This war concerns us directly, and it is up to Province I to fight it."

"But it's crazy! Province P should know we too are a colony..."

"I don't remember asking for your opinion."

Julia breathed out, finding herself standing without having realized she had jumped up from the chair. A ripple on her jaw indicated she was clenching her teeth, but she lowered her eyes to hide her irritation and all-too-obvious feelings.

Yrenes' voice continued, calmer, colder.

"Furthermore, fighting this war could bring interesting advantages to our province."

Julia didn't answer, staring at her hands, now clenched on the precious desk.

"You are going to face the champion of Province P in the duel. You have 40 hours to prepare yourself."

"What?"

Julia abruptly raised her head, finding herself staring from above in the impassive gaze of the Supervisor.

"You heard me. You will face their champion in a duel, as the representative of the Empire and of our province."

"... but why not some military? I don't have the training, if he's a professional fencer he will just massacre me..."

Yrenes raised an eyebrow.

"They appointed a civilian, so we'll have to do the same, otherwise it will look like we fear them. As for the rest, do I have to remind you that you are deployed in the Ministry of Counter-Terrorism? Isn't this enough? You are also the youngest and least experienced in diplomacy, so this makes you objectively the most expendable figure."

Julia's chest heaved slightly, revealing a deep breath, which she struggled to control.

"What if I refused?"

"Your sister's Education Permit will not be renewed, and she will be left alone to face the shame of your choice. You will be subject to Court-Martial, considering we are now at war. You will be tried and judged immediately as a deserter and traitor. Then you will be shot by firing squad. In the back."

A high potential electric shock courses through Julia, while a stone drops in her chest and all color goes

away – electricity reaches the tip of trembling fingers, trembling all the way to the wrist despite clenched fists, then returns up in a flush of blood that from a moment of cold, cold silence lights up again the frenzied drums of the heart.

Nostrils slightly dilated, expressionless lips in a ghostly white face.

"I'll need the recordings of this man's encounters in order to study his moves."

Smug little smile by Yrenes.

"A study room has already been set up in the basement gym."

&

Alone, she sat down on the floor of a huge room furnished with mirrors, staring at the ceiling, knees tucked against her chest and head abandoned against the wall. She barely turned her eyes at the appearance of a blonde cloud at the door, then limited herself to a slight tilt of her head in a small arch and a sad smile.

Such was her condition when Cleo found her. Ignoring the sofa set up in a corner, in front of a still whirring 3D projector, she sat on the floor next to her sister, fixing her bright gaze on Julia's listless eyes.

"I learned of the duel from the loudspeakers on the Stairs. I ran here as soon as possible. I convinced them to allow me to see you."

A small silky hand slapping down on Yrenes' precious writing table.
"Do you want her to win this duel?"
"Of course. Saving ourselves a war is in our interest."
"Then you'll let me speak with her."

"Thank you for coming."

Julia's smile was a painful flash. She sighed and bowed her head to stare at some spot on the floor between her knees, hiding tears that were risking to overflow.

"If I didn't have you, I'd probably just let them shoot me and get it over with. I saw the recordings of some of this Maxim's encounters. He'll tear me to pieces."

Cleo's hand grabbed her sister's shoulder, forcing her to raise her chin and meet her eye.

"Listen to me. You are going to face this Maxim and you will beat him."

"24 years old, a wife, two kids. I saw his declarations of war. He believes in what he's doing, they didn't force him, he's sure he's going to win."

"Very well, you'll defeat him using his overconfidence."

Julia sighed her doubts, but Cleo was already going on with her reasoning.

"He might be an athlete who does nothing but fencing encounters for work, but you have more experience in real combat. The duel that awaits you isn't going to be a sports competition."

At last, a spark lit up in the blue eyes.

"Are you telling me that if I play dirty we're going to play on equal ground?"

"Exactly."

❦

-36 hours to the encounter. Cleo was right. Flashing thoughts occupied Julia's mind, along with disconnected snapshots of recordings and past duels, while the skillful hands of a chiropractor labored on the knots of stress clenching the muscles on her back.

Julia Dream

As much as she was trying to collaborate with the boy that was applying - with great deference - all his art to support the physical condition of the Champion of the Empire before the duel, Julia was aware of the involuntary twitching of her body as she went through the sequences of lunges and parries that paraded in her mind. Again, and again.

Her adversary's stance was impeccable, but a sporting stance, and his own popularity now played against Maxim, as long as she could resist the pressure of his intimidating skill. On her side, Julia could count the fact that she was unknown in the sporting world and that her experience, however limited, was related to actual combat dueling. That, and her being left-handed.

"My lady, would you like to rest for a while? I can dampen the lights, if you wish."

Julia found herself answering to the chiropractor with a slight delay, surprised by the question and the title. Nobody had ever called her "my lady".

"Not now, thank you."

She jumped off the impromptu doctor's lounger with a determined gesture that nonetheless betrayed just how tired she was, as if the obvious tension on her waxen face wasn't revealing enough. She closed her eyes and slowly breathed out, raising her arms above her head, grabbing her wrists and arching her back, appreciating the chiropractor's work.

"My lady, I wanted to tell you it has been an honor for me to work with you today, for such an important task. Your courage will avoid us a war, and I wanted to express the gratitude of a simple citizen of our province."

Julia snapped her half-closed eyes open, really paying attention to the chiropractor for the first time. He was young, younger than her, and sincere admiration shone in his eyes.

Once again she had to stare at the ground to hide her tears.

∞

"How is your study going?"

Julia stopped her sword in mid air, snapping around at the sound of Yrenes' voice and trying to hide her annoyance at being caught unawares by the Supervisor's arrival.

"I'm not going to change my mind, if this is what you want to know. You build your chains well."

Yrenes endured the blow without reacting.

Julia Dream

"Let's sit down a moment. I've brought you some food."

A small table had been mounted next to the couch and the 3D projector. On it, several bottles of water, some of them already emptied by Julia during her training session. Yrenes placed a small transparent box next to them.

The girl slumped on the sofa and examined the pills in box, a triangle and a square of purplish color. She lifted the square in her fingers, a painful gesture considering the quivering of the muscles of her arm and wrist.

"They look different."

"They have been integrated to help you in your task. More vitamins, more minerals."

The Supervisor's explanation received an unconvinced face as an answer, but Counter-Terrorist Mayne grabbed one of the bottles and gulped down the pills as usual. Seconds later she was leaning with her hands on the pillows of the couch, as if fighting a sudden dizziness.

"What did you give me?"

She was gasping, the fury in her voice somehow suffocated by panic and approaching sleep, that was forcing her to close her eyes. Yrenes was calmly getting up.

"Eight hours of sleep. We can't afford you losing your wits because of excessive fatigue."

Julia Dream

Julia's gaze flashed a lightning of hate, then her eyelids closed and didn't open again. Her head fell back on the armrest, and with a bored look on her face Yrenes gestured to the Ministry doctor, who had been waiting at the doorstep, to adjust her decently on the sofa. The Champion of the Empire was not to get up with muscular contractions due to a wrong sleeping posture.

✍

"I want to go out and see the stars. I hope you don't plan on drugging me tonight as well."

Yrenes' office, -10 hours to the duel.

"No, the drug's consequences on the performance of the reflexes is not predictable. You may go."

The Supervisor pushed the little box placed on her writing table, carrying its burden of pills, in Julia's direction: always purple, but both triangular.

"You can choose whether you are going to provide to your alimentation on your own, or if you are going to force me to call medical personnel to have you take in the substances you need."

Julia Dream

Julia clenched her teeth and swallowed the pills, with slow movements of barely restrained fury. She deliberately let the empty bottle she had been drinking from fall noisily on the floor, then crushed it under her boot with controlled violence; finally, she picked it up and threw it in the recycling can, marking every gesture.

"Very well. May I go now?"

Only a slight ripple on Yrenes' forehead betrayed the shadow of an emotion in the Supervisor's composure.

"Permission granted."

Julia marched out of the building without a word or a salute, walking head-down across the corridors all the way to the main entrance of the Ministry - two soldiers were guarding the exit. They snapped to attention as she passed by, following her at a distance until she stopped in the middle of the clearing in front of the building.

The elder of the two answered her questioning look.

"We are your escort, my lady."

Julia was watching them and the barrels of their guns with sad eyes.

"Do you think I'm going to run away?"

"We don't think anything, my lady."

"Right. Yrenes thinks so, and she's not going to risk anything unexpected."

Julia looked up, not expecting an answer. The sky was finally clear, and she found herself breathing deeply the fresh smell of the wind on what was potentially her last night.

She held on to the plan she had worked out, her only shield against an otherwise sure death sentence. Cleo was right – she would have to stick to that idea, without hesitation.

Slightly ahead, she could see the place of the encounter, where seats had been appointed for the war functionaries who were going to assist to the duel. She felt her guts clenching. She remained thoughtful, her hands on her abdomen, taming her breath and her heart until the stars faded and the horizon turned blue.

She turned back only after the first ray of the rising sun had caressed her forehead.

∽

"The functionaries are signing the papers. Maxim is already in the waiting room."

Julia Dream

Julia was donning the blouse of the shiny white outfit that marked her as a direct representative of the Emperor. Embroidered on her back she bore the crest with the symbol of the Imperial Black Moon, stylized to show all its phases.

She closed her eyes for a moment, stroking the fresh and smooth fabric, so different from anything she had ever worn before.

"Fasten the sword on my left side."

Yrenes knelt down to second Julia's request, keeping quiet despite her disapproving look - the temporary hierarchy of the duel placed the Champion of the Empire way above a simple Supervisor.

"You should meet Maxim in the waiting room. After that, you'll be escorted on the field by different entrances."

Julia nodded, heading with outward calm towards the Ministry Hall, her head held high. She recognized immediately the man she had studied in the 3D projections: Maxim was, as predicted, shapely, blondish and sufficiently sure of himself to show off a relaxed posture, sitting on a wide crimson velvet armchair in the waiting room.

Yrenes silently left, leaving the two contenders on their own.

"So, you're the slave the Empire has sent to do the dirty job?"

The girl merely stared at Maxim in silence. He softened his tone.

"I'm sorry for you, you know. What did you do to deserve this death sentence?"

Maxim sat up on the armchair, placing his elbows on the armrests and lowering his voice.

"If you're not going to resist, I'll make it quick. You'll become a symbol of rebellion against the oppression of the Empire, a hero and a martyr revered in all of Province P."

Julia raised her chin to better look down on him.

"Province P – of which I couldn't care less – will have no independence, no matter the result of this farce of a duel. You have a wife and two children, you can still pull back. The Empire won't deem you personally responsible for the rebellion."

The man stood up as well, looking at her with contempt.

"You don't understand, do you? I'm here because I decided to serve a cause, unlike you, and not because I was forced to. And that is why I will win."

Julia's metallic gaze caught the hazel eyes of her adversary, and suddenly Maxim read in her stare such hate and savagery that he recoiled, trying to hide his retreat by turning his back on her.

The steely voice of the Champion of the Empire met him anyway.

"You are the one who does not understand."

They waited in silence for the signal to begin.

∽

Black and white flags singing their promises of glory to the wind, in the solid blue of an unreal sky. She doesn't see Cleo, she doesn't see Yrenes, she doesn't notice the Emperor and the arrayed aristocracy, she doesn't hear the nervous public fidgeting in the makeshift seats.

Julia's senses are all for the enemy, closing in on the field of the encounter.

She draws with a slow, deliberate gesture of her right hand - the sword flashes in the pale morning sun. Maxim closes in, his grace ever so slightly cracked by a feigned confidence.

Julia waits. Maxim starts the dance, circles around his prey - eyes locked on each other.

Then Julia's sword leaves her right hand, sends a golden flash in the morning wind, draws an arch of light with its course, and ends in the confident grip of the left hand - dodging below and well beyond the surprised attack of her adversary, the Champion of the Empire sweeps her blade a few inches from the ground, strikes down the enemy's footing, slashing through sinew and bone of the ankle, forcing the knee to bend, as drops begin to fall on the sand.

Maxim falls face-down, Julia already behind him - holding it with both hands, she sinks her blade in his back. Again, and again - until she just leaves it there, stuck somewhere in his ribcage.

She averts her eyes from the widening pool of blood, faces a muted audience with fiery eyes. Checks on her enemy - he won't get up.

Without even recovering her sword, long strides take her out of the arena.

"Very good Mayne, I always knew you would win!"
She avoids a gloating Yrenes. Ignores the small crowd of spectators gathering to meet and congratulate her, only to shrink away at her gaze, and rushes in the arms of a slim figure making her way through the functionaries using agility and elbows.
A moment of stiff astonishment, then Julia melts in her sister's embrace.
"Cleo... Let's go home."

II

Julia was lying curled up on the bed, eyes closed, her breathing slow and regular - but she was not sleeping. The light of the sunset filtered through shutters and eyelids, and the heavy sensation much like lead which she now felt in muscle and sinew didn't allow her mind to simply turn itself off as she would have liked. She rolled on her back, with a grunt of pain at the movement, finding herself staring at the ceiling, her arms sprawled in the attempt to ease some muscular pain.

The ring of the videophone shattered the brief relaxation of her posture. Although they were the only ones that weren't hurting, Julia felt her facial muscles contracting in an expression that from worry, quickly relaxed into simple annoyance - the line had not opened itself automatically, so it couldn't be a ministerial call.

Without hurrying too much, she stretched one hand toward the videophone to open audio communication, ignoring the video for the moment.

"Who's there?"

"This is Secretary Marcus, of the Advanced Corps of the Army. I would like to speak to the Champion of the Empire Mayne."

There was no arrogance in the voice that resonated in the room, simply educated self-confidence. Julia rose from the bed, sitting on the edge and opening the video function of the communicator on the wall: on the small gray screen she saw the face of a handsome man with gray hair, looking at her with deep brown eyes. She answered neutrally, pushing backwards some strands of hair that had fallen in front of her face.

"It's me, nice to meet you. May I ask the reason behind the honor of this call?"

The Secretary addressed her with a small smile.

"Ever thought of a career improvement?"

Julia remained silent, the expression in her eyes betraying the struggle between a wish for change and the deep distrust of those who have only seen their life change for the worse.

The man seemed to detect this conflict and continued talking, without changing his friendly tone.

"I have a proposal, and would like to meet you in my study to discuss it."

"Now?"

"I was thinking about tomorrow, around noon. I have already spoken with the Ministry, you have been assigned a free day. I suggest you rest tonight, I would say you need it after your impressive feat."

Julia nodded, surprised by the kindness in these words.

"You have my thanks. Where can I find you?

"Escalator 7, first villa on the right. See you tomorrow!"

◈

"You're restless."

Cleo was staring at the ceiling, in the darkness of the room lit only by the slight luminescence of the videophone. Next to her, Julia's irregular shape was tossing and turning in the useless quest for a position that could facilitate sleep. The Champion of the Empire sighed, turning on her stomach and peeking at her sister.

"Too many things happening all together. I don't know what this Marcus guy wants from me."

Cleo shook her head gently, turning around to look at the darker shadow at her side.

"I don't know. The Marcus family is old and close to the Emperor, for what I know."

Julia breathed out slowly, forcing her willpower to relax at least some of her aching muscles.

"Interesting. I'll try to be nicer than I was with Yrenes."

"That coward deserved it."

The ice in Cleo's voice surprised Julia, who spread out one hand to find and squeeze her sister's.

"What's important is that it's over."

Cleo answered the squeeze on her hand, lowering her misty eyes to then look back at Julia, choking back tears.

"Yes, it's going to be fine. The ways of this Marcus seem different from Yrenes'."

"I'm scared by the fact he would ask rather than order."

Cleo wrinkled her forehead in a thoughtful expression.

"Well, it's similar to when they put our study group to the test, asking us to express an opinion. You're free to be judged by your choices; it's a different kind of bond."

"So Marcus is putting me through some kind of test?"

"So it would seem."

Julia flexed the muscles of her legs, stretching her feet and then extending her heels, then reserving the same treatment to her shoulders before slumping back down on the pillow. She then answered with a new, strange serenity of sorts.

"Well, I guess that tomorrow I'll find out what kind of trap Secretary Marcus has laid out for me."

And then she abruptly gave in to sleep.

◈

The sun glistened in innumerable shimmers on the fragments of glass trapped in the black concrete of the escalators, so much that Julia closed her eyes for a second, compressing the world in nothing more than warmth on her skin, the buzz of the escalators and the breeze in her hair.

Her climb towards Marcus' villa was basically solitary – although occasionally she crossed some students descending the escalator. As she ascended, the horizon and the color of the city itself changed: the bright green of the aristocratic districts recalled, in tamer and more controlled hues, the emerald of the endless Forest beyond the Walls.

Below, at the lower level of the city, a group of people was talking with the garrison of the North Gate, who briefly opened the doors for the small procession. Julia shivered. Civilians only ventured out of the City, always escorted, for funerals.

Looking back up, she noticed she had almost reached her destination. The escalator ended in the last scaffolding, leading to the terrace hosting the villas of the northern side of the city. Following Marcus' directions, Julia headed right, finding herself in front of the gate and walls of an aristocratic mansion.

The doors opened upon her arrival, proving that Marcus had already requested from the Imperial database Julia's ID code to grant her access. A guest in Villa Marcus, she found herself following a path lined with trees, set in an unnatural silence, where the only noise was a vague and distant splashing of water and the call of the birds hidden in the foliage.

Julia considered the villa with a feeling of growing discomfort. Cleo had described similar environments, but the unusual presence of trees and animals, even if distant, contributed to increasing the hesitation in her steps. She walked as in a trance, hypnotized by the rustling of the leaves, up to the entrance of the house, a rectangular block of marble decorated with columns that reminded Julia of the architectural majesty of the Ministry of Counter-Terrorism.

A glass double door, listed in metal, silently opened at her arrival, and a voice, which Julia recognized as that of Secretary Marcus, called from the end of the corridor that lead from the entrance to a sharp turn on the left.

"Please, come in. Join me."

Past the entrance, sun rays on the soft carpet of the corridor, the sheer luxury of the polished wooden floor, the elegance of finely rounded corners. And by far more pervasive and perturbing, the undetermined sound embracing the environment, rhythmical and yet varied.

Julia stops at the center of the corridor for a moment, looks for a source - only a glimmer in a corner of the ceiling. The sound seems to fade, then returns, insists, vanishes again in its mysterious hole.

Baffled, Julia turns the corner to meet the Secretary.

"Well met!"

A tall, smiling man, elegant in his decorated uniform. He stood up to greet her upon her arrival, extending a hand she shook with barely concealed suspicion.

"Please, have a seat."

Julia sat down mechanically at the edge of one of the chairs opposite the Secretary's desk. She noticed that Marcus' gaze followed her gestures carefully, but when their eyes met, he immediately smiled at her, almost winking.

"I believe I can skip the pleasantries and proceed with my proposal."

Julia blushed, embarrassed by his observation.

"I had no intention of being rude, I truly apologize. I don't know the adequate protocols of behavior for this situation."

The Secretary's reaction surprised her once again, for Marcus was giggling heartily.

"No violation in etiquette or protocol, don't worry."

His tone then became serious once again, as he raised his eyes from the desk to look at Julia in eye.

"I would like you to join the Advanced Corps of the Imperial Army."

Julia arched her eyebrows in surprise.

"Mr. Secretary, I have no military rank whatsoever..."

"No matter. I have full liberty to decide who I want to recruit for the training program."

"... and you believe I could be a good fit for this position?"

"You wouldn't be here otherwise. Your experience in the diplomatic field is sufficient, and I believe you have widely proved your skill in the recent battle with Province P... Champion of the Empire Mayne."

"And my sister?"

"Level I Education Permit."

The girl remained in silence for a few moments, counting her accelerated heartbeats, rapid thoughts fleeting like clouds in her blue gaze.

"You could order the Ministry to issue my immediate transfer. Why bother with my opinion?"

"The Army supports the Empire. The Advanced Corps supports the Army. The task is too important to use enforcement as a surrogate for motivation."

He leaned towards her, placing his elbows on the desk and joining his fingertips.

"Perhaps a couple of considerations could help your decision."

Julia tenses, ready for the familiar talk of very thinly veiled threats - yet Marcus' tone is steady.

"You can remain at the Ministry, with a Supervisor you hate and who fears and hates you in return, until (casually, of course) a duel to the first blood will go too far, thus ending your career and your life. Or you can decide to come with me, and risk new dangers and prizes."

Julia is holding her breath, exhales, forces herself into a more relaxed posture.

A piercing look from Marcus.

"What then, of my proposal?"

"I accept."

"Good!"

The Secretary pulled out a paper from a folder resting between the documents piled high on the desk, handing over to Julia a pen so that she could sign the contract. Julia quickly read and signed, feeling for a moment as if she had just signed her own death warrant.

Marcus' smiling voice interrupted her thoughts.

"No use in reminding you that from this moment, you are now part of the Imperial Army and subject to martial law. Questions?"

Stopping to think, she realized that the sound she had heard at the entrance had never stopped, always changing yet similar, intrusive and fascinating at the same time.

"Yes. What is this sound?"

"Excellent question."

The Secretary appeared favorably impressed.

"It's music. It interacts with the emotional sphere. You will study some of its applications, and we'll talk about it more if you're interested. By the way, just call me Marcus. I'll be your tutor in the first phase of your training."

"Would you mind another question... Marcus?"

"Not at all."

"I thought that wisdom was measured by one's control over her feelings."

"Clearly. And yet you have to know your emotions to control them."

The girl pondered for a moment on this answer, her frown a clear indicator of her reflection. Marcus stood up, immediately followed by Julia who understood that the Secretary was now dismissing her.

"Very well. We're leaving in two days. I'll formalize your new position with the Ministry of Counter-Terrorism."

"Thank you."

Julia's answer slipped from her lips with an almost inappropriate speed that underlined her relief, and once again the Secretary smiled at her, this time with a strange glow in his eye – sadness? Irony perhaps?

"Don't worry about it. You'll have time to thank me."

❦

The propellers of the aerovehicle whirred with a circular and constant sound. From the window Julia watched as the landing platform and the city became smaller and smaller. She was looking for her block and the window where she imagined Cleo would be staring at the sky, as if searching for her sister, who was now flying into the pink-colored clouds of dawn.

"So you're leaving?"

Julia nods, looking away from Cleo's sad eyes.

"I'll have permits to visit you, and three videophone calls before my first day off."

Julia Dream

The shadow of a worried smile on the younger girl's face.

"This is what you want, right?"

"I don't want to rot in the Ministry with Yrenes. And you deserve to carry on with your studies."

Cleo squeezes her sister's hand in silence.

The rhythmical cluck of the aerovehicle propeller slowed down to a stop, giving way to the low buzz of the electromagnetic engines.

"Well, we're in for a bit of silence for a few hours, before we start landing maneuvers."

Marcus had commented happily, adjusting on his seat and stretching his legs forward.

"Where are we going?"

Julia was watching eagerly the green stretch of the Forest, which extended as far as she could see.

The Secretary gave her an encouraging smile.

"Province R, Training Base n. 3"

And then the land ended, and the bright green of the trees became a deep blue, etched with countless dimples and facets, at times brilliant with the gold of the reflected light of the sun on the surface of the water. For a while, small green islands and archipelagos animated the blue, then white and translucent little clouds, pierced by the rays of the sun, yet still capable of casting small darker shadows on the shimmering gem of the sea.

Julia brought a hand to her chest, struck by a sudden and invasive feeling, like the inexplicable tears which suddenly filled her eyes.

"From the few holograms I had seen, I had never imagined the sea could be so beautiful."

She spoke with a choked voice, keeping her face to the window; she didn't want Marcus to know she was crying.

The Secretary was looking at her with half-closed eyes.

"It can be terrible, up close."

Julia pressed her forehead to the window, staring below and quickly pulling herself together. She frowned, disquieted. The incredible view had a strange effect on her, and it also reminded her of something.

"Are you ok?"

She opened her eyes wide at the sound of Marcus' voice, and turned around to look at him. She had found a connection in her mind, even if she didn't know how to explain it.

"Yes. I couldn't place my finger on it at first, but for some reason the sea makes me think of music."

Marcus looked at her, cocking his head to one side and smiling slightly.

"Really?"

She didn't answer, not knowing how to interpret his tone of voice. The sea stretch was ending, breaking with long waves on a shore with golden sand. The Forest started again ahead, but Julia had the impression she could see a brown scar in the thick carpet of trees.

The Secretary stretched the muscles of his legs and his arms, weaving his fingers and extending his hands in front of his chest to hyper-extend his shoulders.

"We're almost there."

Julia guessed the space she had seen could be the base, but the aerovehicle flew past it, keeping at distance - after a couple of minutes Julia realized the base was much bigger. Ahead of them solar panels placed on the rooftops of the buildings shone like mirrors, and high walls separated the base from the Forest, as did a ring of deforested zone beyond the doors, just like in cities.

She heard the propeller of the aerovehicle gain momentum, while the pilot deactivated the electromagnetic engine to avoid interference with the machinery of the base: the buildings were arranged to allow the landing of the aerovehicle at the center of the structure.

Marcus pointed to a flat and long building to their right.

"Those are the student dorms. You have been assigned a room, you'll find clothes and gear. When you're ready, we'll take a tour of RTB3."

She nodded, concentrated.

"And we'll begin your training. With something light, for today."

∽

Still studying her new quarters, Julia tied the last strap of her rigid plastiresin glove on her left forearm, testing the mobility of her fingers with a few of movements of the hand, before stopping for a moment in front of the mirror. The small room was minimal, but comfortable. In a small closet she had found the clothes she was now wearing, and on the wall opposite the door hung the mirror where she was now contemplating her new looks.

Julia Dream

She was surprised by her image, dressed in the military green uniform. She had donned the trousers easily (they were loose on the legs, thick but lighter compared to ministerial synthetic fabric) along with the tight, bright green long-sleeved shirt which bore the identification badge on the right shoulder. It was harder to correctly adjust the body armor.

The bodice in dark green plastiresin was tied with groups of intersecting grapples asymmetrically located along the back and sides while on the inside other hooks, invisible from the outside, connected the bodice of the armor to the belt and the rays departing from the protective necklace to the central cuirass. Elastic straps connected the shoulders to the reinforced gloves, keeping them in place without squeezing the forearms.

Julia put to a test the elasticity of the glove, rotating her wrist, and observed her clenched fist with satisfaction, as the complex system of foils on the joints proved efficient in granting mobility.

The overall effect of the uniform was impressive, as she stared in the mirror; her face looked even younger, in contrast with her warlike attire.

Soldier Mayne stretched her shoulders and her neck, pulling her arms up, then lowering them at her side as she vaguely nodded at her reflection, with a thin smile of understanding. Her training had begun from the moment she had donned her new uniform: it was heavy.

She went out to join Marcus, who was waiting for her in the open space at the center of the base. The sun was shining in its warmest hour, and Julia was quite surprised by the number of people coming and going. In the city only students and some functionaries were not in office during day hours.

The Secretary followed her gaze.

"They're going to lunch."

Julia looked at him without understanding, but he turned around, heading towards a dirt path which led to the back entrance of a squat building in front of them, on the other side of the open space. Soldiers of different ranks were going in and out of the main entrance, but Marcus went straight to the back door.

Behind a window, a soldier with a bored face snapped to attention as Marcus drew near. The Secretary pulled out a document of some sort from his pocket and the two men exchanged words Julia didn't hear, from her respectful distance - then the soldier handed Marcus a small object which looked like some kind of green sphere.

Turning towards her, Marcus suddenly threw the object in Julia's direction, who caught it mid-air.

"Well, well."

The man was smiling at her increasing perplexity, but appeared satisfied with her reflexes. She opened her fingers to contemplate the object she was now holding. Its surface was smooth, light green in color, a few shades paler than the grass; however from up close she noticed its shape wasn't a precise sphere, also because in a small dent, a brown petiole betrayed its organic nature.

Curious, Julia turned the thing in her hands.

"What is it?"

"It's a fruit, an apple."

Marcus had now reached her and unceremoniously sat down on a huge flat boulder coming out of the thin vegetation growing between the base buildings and the wall.

"Your classmates are eating, but you can't join them yet because you don't have the right physical preparation. Approaching biological nutrition is one of the first teachings we provide our military."

"Biological nutrition?"

Julia was shocked. She sat on the boulder next to the Secretary.

"I thought it was a legacy of the past..."

Marcus shook his head, dead serious.

"Oh no. It's important that certain categories of society, such as the military, don't lose completely their natural inclination for a biological nutrition."

"But why? Aren't synthesis pills more practical?"

"You won't find synthetic food should you lose yourself in the Forest. Our army, and even more so the Advanced Corps, have to know how to survive in any reasonable condition."

He watched her as she stared at the apple, smiling his small sly smile.

"You'll notice you actually develop a taste for this kind of nutrition, after a while."

Julia stopped looking at the fruit to look at her guide, her slightly arched eyebrows revealing her thoughts.

"And where is biological food grown?"

"In the villas of the chemical aristocracy, of course. Chemical and biochemical, we could say."

Marcus stood up, while Julia pondered on these words, and stopped her with a quick gesture of an open hand.

"Stay here with your apple - I have some things to do, I'll be back in a while. Try to eat all of it, but you can throw the core away."

He smiled at her encouragingly.

"And don't worry should you feel a little sick, it's normal."

Julia stared at the apple for a few seconds, weighing it with caution; at last she sunk her teeth in the thin and light pulp of the fruit.

She closes her eyes, frowns as the sour juice strikes the unsuspecting taste gums. The structure of the apple gives in and the morsel is ripped off, trapped in the grasp of her teeth. Chewing is slow, clumsy; rich in grimacing, while completely new impressions flow on her concentrated face.

Her gums were already aching as she found herself swallowing, and soon after the first bite, she felt an unusual quiver in her abdomen. She instinctively placed a hand on her stomach, finding the semi-rigid surface of her armor; however her belly didn't signal new turmoil.

Julia Dream

Once again, she focused on the apple and attacked it with another bite, which left on the greenish pulp the reddish marks of fresh blood. Julia kept on chewing, ignoring the stinging and the pain, obeying her orders and exploring the possibilities of an entirely new sense. A simple apple revealed itself salty in the peel, sour in the juice and sweet in aftertaste - and crisp and tough in the core, which she found quite easy to discover.

She was about to finish the apple when she was taken by a feeling of stifling pressure on her ribcage - she realized her forehead was beaded with sweat, when she stopped to breathe. A shiver ran under her skin, then she had to bend in two on the axis of her lower belly, as if struck by an invisible crowbar. She recognized in the cramp the symptom of the pain to come.

She looked at the last morsel of apple she still held in her hand, then gulped it down with a challenging stare.

≈

The afternoon sun was starting its descent when Julia began mandatory training.

"Let's start running three loops."

Julia Dream

Instructor Skintilla was a young girl on the short side, but muscular and authoritative, tanned on her arms and face. She wore no conventional armor or uniform and sported her instructor rank pinned on the chest of her tank top.

Together with the other Advanced Corps recruits (she counted more or less 15), Julia obeyed, sprinting down the path which led to the dirt route encompassing the inside perimeter of the walls of the base. She started off armed with good will and enthusiasm, and by the time she arrived where the three loops were supposed to begin, she was already tired and aware of her mistake.

Considerably slowing down in an attempt to correct her effort, she let the others pass her hoping that a more measured pace would bring her accelerated heartbeat to a sustainable rhythm; to no avail. She found herself lagging last and far behind the others even before the end of the first loop.

Her armor was heavy, her legs were starting to ache and the air itself seemed to scorch her lungs, expanded by the effort.

"You can remain at the Ministry, with a Supervisor you hate and which fears and hates you in return, until (casually, of

course) a duel to the first blood will go too far thus ending
your career and your life. Or you can decide to come with
me, and risk new dangers and prizes."

She gritted her teeth at the memory of Marcus' words, and
found herself half-way in the intended route, with a small
cloud of dust ahead of her indicating the position of her
classmates. Even if late, she joined with them after
completing the three required loops, sweating and
breathless.

Ignoring the jeering smirks which were lighting up the
faces of her colleagues, she limited her actions to a gesture
of salute to the Instructor, carefully listening to what she
had to say. Skintilla had observed the group while they
were running and was now sharing her observations,
while renewing the knot that kept her long red hair in
place.

"You tire too early because you burn energies when you
don't need to, and you don't have any sense of time. This
time you're going to run five loops, but with an element in
your favor."

Julia had forced herself to remain impassible and regain
breath, but raised an eyebrow in surprise when at a sign

by Skintilla the entire base echoed with a modulated sound, different yet similar to what she had heard for the first time in Marcus' studio: music.

It filled the ears and the vibrations echoed in her chest, reminding Julia of the relentlessness of the Escalators of the City, of the strength and beauty of the sea she had seen from the aerovehicle, of the solemn welcoming parade in honor of the Emperor.

She found herself running close to the group of her classmates, her breathing regulated by the powerful and rhythmical timing of the music, and after three loops she hadn't lost them yet, despite her fatigue. At the fourth loop she decided she wasn't going to quit. Even though by now she was literally dragging her feet, she let her focus follow the musical guide, and arrived at the end of the fifth loop without a substantial delay.

She didn't see Skintilla's curious glance because she was doubled up, trying to catch her breath, and barely noticed the Instructor's voice announcing the end of the warm up, ordering the group to move to the gym.

"That's enough, Mayne!"

Skintilla's powerful voice, nervous and amazed.

With a wild flick of her head, Julia moves out of the way a lock of hair that had fallen on her face, lingers for in a moment in the stance that sees her hands intent on flattening down her opponent, a knee well planted on his breastbone. Only a moment, then she lets go of the grip on his neck, leaving visible red finger marks on his wrist as well, where the other hand had caught him.

She gets up without a word, placing herself respectfully in line.

"We could say you have drastically underestimated your opponent, Kob."

The instructor's voice was flat and final.

"The lesson is over for today. You may go."

A flash of her golden eyes.

"Mayne, stay for a moment."

Her face courteously blank, her breath barely accelerated, Julia waited for the reprimand to come. Skintilla paused for a moment in considering her new student, head tilted backwards, hands on her hips.

"Do you know why you made a mistake?"

"I guess I exaggerated."

The Instructor relaxed her stance and nodded, hearing a note of regret in the girl's otherwise blank voice.

"Yes, but not for the reasons you think."

Something clicked in Julia's eyes, which became more present, as if the situation had encountered a shift in its nature, from abstract to tangible.

"Kob deserved this lesson, he'll be fine with some bruises and next time he'll think twice before seeking to humiliate a classmate."

Julia looked at Skintilla with amazement, surprised by these words, while the Instructor went on with her explanation.

"You made a mistake because you exaggerated in your passion, you didn't study, you didn't calculate, you performed your action with enthusiasm, certainly, but against any Terrorist you would have lost, surely."

The girl bowed her head.

"I thought I had my determination in check."

"Not enough. I could read your anger between the lines... and not only the present one."

Skintilla's voice was kind, but her student twitched. The Instructor softened her voice.

"You must always remember that our enemies are considerably stronger and quicker than us... an impulsive approach like yours with Kob would be suicidal."

Julia remained in silence, but her unsettled face showed she had understood. Skintilla nodded, at least partially satisfied by the girl's tacit approval, and smiled at her.

"I believe we have understood each other. Remember my words! You may go now."

❦

Free from the weight of the armor, Julia let herself collapse on the camp bed in her room. The sun had set and she now was appreciating her resting time before a new day of training. She relaxed her tired muscles for some minutes, before rolling on one side in the direction of the videophone, where she dialed her home number.

"Hello?"

Cleo's tired and suspicious voice echoed in the room, bringing Julia to a smile.

"Hello Cleo, it's me!"

The video opened up almost immediately, showing the happy and relieved expression on the blonde girl's face.

"Julia, how are you? Where are you?"

"I'm fine. Somewhere in province R, I've been told."

Julia paused for a moment, remembering her trip in the aerovehicle. That was about 14 hours ago, expanded in her perception of time.

"I saw the sea coming here! It's really hard to describe..."

Cleo widened her eyes, curious.

"I can imagine! For the rest, how is the place?"

"Full of trees, but not too different from the Forest we see from the City. Actually, I wanted to ask you something. What do you know of the Terrorists?"

There was a small pause before Cleo's thoughtful image answered her question.

"Not much, history isn't my field, but I can do some research if you want."

Julia shook her head.

"No, don't worry about it. What can you tell me, for now?"

Cleo answered slowly, while extracting information from the depths of her memory.

"I know they are a result of the Cataclysm. The Empire has always fought them to defend its borders. We take no prisoners. They live in the Forest, throughout the whole Empire."

"In what sense, they are a result of the Cataclysm?"

Cleo shrugged.

"I wouldn't know how to say more. I only know that the very first City Walls and other fortifications in the Empire were made at the time of the Cataclysm, and that the Walls exist to defend the citizens from the Terrorists."

"So there must be some kind of link between them and the Cataclysm, you suggest? It makes sense."

The girl on the other side of the videophone smiled, somewhat sadly. A veil of worry shadowed her eyes.

"I don't want to know why you're asking me."

❧

The following morning, the scheduled lesson was Theory of Ministerial Communication - however, Julia found Marcus waiting for her outside her room. He was distractedly playing with an apple, tossing it in the air and picking it up again, and at the sight of the fruit she found herself subconsciously passing her tongue on her gums, still scratched and aching from the day before.

The Secretary beckoned her to follow him.

"Come, you don't need the theory. We have other gaps to fill."

Julia noticed that instead of his usual city uniform, Marcus was wearing a black plastiresin armor very similar to hers, and that a couple of objects very much like grenades dangled from his waist.

"We're going in the Forest for our lesson. I don't think we'll have to fight, since we'll stay close to the walls, but it's best to take the necessary precautions."

The girl widened her eyes, but made no further concession to her anxiety.

"And should we meet something, will stunning grenades work?"

"Ha, you recognized them! You were well instructed in the Ministry. They're going to be enough since we're not going far, they should create the commotion we'll eventually need to retreat."

As he spoke, Marcus had started heading towards the northern side of the base, where the walls sported a thick metal gate. From one of the guarding towers at its side, a soldier saluted the Secretary and initiated the procedure required to open the doors. The two metallic shutters opened with the whirr of EM engines, just enough to let two figures through, before closing again with a loud clang.

The barren ring without trees stretched in front of them, with a path heading directly into the lush green. Julia paused for a second to observe intensely the deep shadow of the Forest, her nose slightly turned upwards to catch the unusual scent of the surroundings.

Marcus pointed with his hand to a spot ahead of them, bordering the woods.

"See that clearing? It looks like a good place for breakfast."

He slapped the apple in her hand and headed towards the forest with quick strides, leaving Julia no other option than to follow him.

From up close the trees no longer looked all the same, actually revealing all their diversity and splendor - some had thick foliage and branches so thin, that they cancelled every fear of hidden dangers. Others were strong enough to harbor a tree-house, while yet another different kind tempted swarms of insects with wide and pulpy flowers.

The passage from the sunny base to the shadow of the thick vegetation marked a considerable difference in temperature - the girl shivered, well aware of her own fear. She could feel the tension rising in her shoulders, and had the unnerving impression of being observed by invisible and inquisitive eyes.

When they arrived to the clearing the Secretary had indicated, Julia found that some rocks had been placed in circle, forming rudimentary seats.

"After you!"

Smiling, Marcus gestured her to sit down and she gingerly placed herself with her back to the base, keeping the Forest in check. In order to hide her apprehension, she sank her teeth in the apple, concentrating on the sting caused by the acid juice of the fruit on the cuts in her mouth.

"I know, it feels awkward the first time. But sooner or later you'll leave on an expedition, and it's fair you see some of the Forest, first."

Julia concluded her slow chewing of the piece of apple.

"Marcus... may I ask a question?"

The Secretary nodded.

"Who, or what, are the Terrorists, exactly?"

Marcus sighed.

"They are people, like us. Only wild after centuries of radiation and decline. If we exclude their extraordinary strength and the fact that they have the yellow eyes of a nocturnal hunter, they are very similar to us."

Julia frowned.

"Did the mutation occur as a consequence of the Cataclysm?"

The Secretary nodded, observing his nails in silence for a couple of moments before speaking again.

"Yes. The disaster was devastating, but not completely unforeseen. The main cities had anti-radiation shielding. Not so for the rest of the territory."

"And the Terrorists are at war with us because they hate us, because we descend from those who left their ancestors to the radiation?"

Marcus shook his head, a bitter smile on his lips.

"Of course not. You think they know history? We clash with them because they are nomadic, and they could often trespass our borders."

Julia shook her head, perplexed.

"Couldn't we re-introduce them to the cities?"

"Unfortunately, that isn't possible. There have been attempts, but they can't stand closed spaces and let themselves die out of sadness. Their heart is too big."

"In what sense?"

"It's a metaphor. When you feel a strong emotion, you can sometimes feel it in your chest - this is why feelings are often associated with the heart."

Her eyes were veiled by a shadow, as if her thoughts had somehow detached from the conversation.

"I know."

Marcus went on, dragging her back to her present lesson.

"During missions, you'll always have to remember that we don't want to destroy the Terrorists, but to keep them away from our borders. We don't know what lies in the deeper Forest."

Julia raised her eyebrows in surprise.

"Are you saying we actually need them?"

"In a certain sense. They are an interposed force between us and the unknown."

"I have another question."

Marcus opened his arms and smiled.

"Tell me."

"Why do we call them Terrorists? They don't seem so terrifying, and yet even the name the Ministry gives them seems to suggest they are a considerable menace."

The Secretary giggled slightly.

"You're right. But the reason for the name has an historical origin. At the time of the Cataclysm, people feared not open war but the surprise attack of groups named "terrorist" because of their strategy of terror, involving attacks on civilian population. In time, "terrorist" became just another word for "enemy". That's why we still speak of Terrorists and Counter-Terrorism."

"Oh."

Julia remained in silence for minutes, pondering the received information and cautiously nibbling at her apple; at last she turned to Marcus once again.

"Are all nobles so educated on pre-Cataclysm history?"

He smiled, winking at her, proving that making her feel ignorant was not his intention.

"Not all of them. Some are more interested in the past than others."

"Good. I would have liked to study more."

She stared at the ground to hide her regret, yet Marcus easily interpreted her voice.

"You already know more than most, and we can follow up on this conversation any time."

After these words, the Secretary looked up at the sky, where dark clouds were rolling in.

"I'd say we have learned enough on the denizens of the Forest, for today. It's time for us to return to the base." Julia stood up, examining the ancient trees with attention and respect. Marcus smiled at her, while rising up from his seat.

"Don't worry. We'll be back."

III

"So the Secretary's pet deigns to sit with us? And why is this?"

Three months had passed since her arrival in the training base. Without flinching, Julia slowly placed the bowl she was holding on the long table where her classmates where sitting. She leveled her gaze to meet Kob's eyes, since he had expressed out loud the question written on the face of everyone present. She issued her answer with ministerial tranquility.

"Up to today, I wasn't ready for a regular biological nutrition. I was filling in my gaps in private."

She sat down, feeling that the tension regarding her was decreasing.

"What regiment do you come from?"

A few chairs away, a voice was speaking up for the general curiosity.

"Actually, I come from the Ministry of Counter-Terrorism, not from the Army."

Concentrating once again on the table and her food, Julia clumsily picked up what she had learned to be a spoon, dipping it in the greenish liquid in her soup bowl. For a moment she stopped to contemplate it, before cautiously bringing the spoon to her lips - she quickly lowered it when the hot soup burned her mouth.

"Mayne, where do you come from?"

At this new question, Julia dropped her spoon and subconsciously started flattening out the folds of her slacks – her hand revealing the stress her face was trying to hide behind a blank expression.

"Province I."

Her interlocutor's face lit up in surprise.

"That's where I come from. Are you the Champion of the Empire Mayne?"

A sudden silence fell over the table, while fifteen gazes converged on Julia.

The smile becomes, if possible, even more embarrassed and stretched, her shoulders sag and Julia's hand grasps the now forgotten spoon almost as if it were a sword.

"Yes, it's me."

Julia Dream

Kob laughed heartily, followed by all of her other classmates. He placed his elbows on the table to get closer, bringing his palm down on the table to accompany his epiphany and following statement.

"So that's why you fight like that! Why didn't you tell us from the start?"

Relief. Julia lowered the spoon, breathing out at the sudden end of the hostilities.

∽

"Julia!"

"Hi Cleo!"

The sisters smiled at each other through the videophone screen.

"How are you? Everything all right?"

Cleo's piercing gaze lingered on the fleeting uncertainty of Julia's smile, on the concern lurking in her eyes.

"Yes, all good. I had a talk with my classmates today, I'm going to start having lunch with them..."

Soldier Mayne unstrapped her armor, slipping out of her technological breastplate and tossing it on the bed before resuming the conversation. She spoke quickly, hiding the embarrassment that had caused this brief pause.

"And then tomorrow we're going into the Forest to look for some Terrorists."

Cleo's pale face became even whiter, if possible, and Julia spoke quickly to answer her sister's silence.

"It shouldn't be dangerous. We are still in training, after all. We're going on a recon mission, not to war."

"But you decided to call me just in case something happens, right?"

It was Julia's turn to remain silent. Cleo forced herself to smile, failed, then tried to draw out her most reassuring tone.

"Don't worry, it's going to be fine."

Her sister answered her words with a smile showing acceptance rather than anxiety, nodding.

"Yes, everything is going to be fine. If you don't have any news tomorrow, you can be sure of it. But how are you?"

Cleo hesitated for a brief moment, as if uncertain about the answer.

"Quite well. I'm dating a planner who works with the Study Center. I met him while he was taking measures of our class for refurnishing. We'll see how it goes."

Julia's smile broadened, lit up with sincere happiness.

"Good! I'm happy for you!"

The blonde girl looked at the time.

"I'm not keeping you up late, am I? I don't want to deprive you of sleep."

"No, don't worry, we're going tomorrow night."

"Ok, ok."

There was a brief pause, then Cleo picked up the topic again, smiling shyly.

"I'm glad you're happy about this."

Julia goggled.

"Of course! Why should I not be happy for you if you're dating someone?"

Cleo shrugged.

"Perhaps because I think Dreas isn't exactly your type."

"Well, you have to like him, not I."

"True."

Julia observed her sister's thoughtful expression, slightly tilting her head on her left shoulder.

"How about you introduce me to him when I come back?"

Cleo smiled, nodding.

"Sure. I'm waiting for you."

Julia Dream

❦

The night was encompassing, tangible. A white curtain of fog rose from the fertile soil of the Forest; the soldiers squinted to accustom their eyes to the darkness and gripped their rifles, even though they weren't allowed to use them.

They walked in the moonlight, ignoring their flashlights for the moment. Julia followed Skintilla's red hair, up at the front of the line: the Instructor moved silently and confidently in the thickening tangle of vegetation. The mist turned any nocturnal noise of the Forest into something disquieting, but those who were startled in the darkness bowed their heads and kept quiet - their orders were to remain silent.

Skintilla finally spoke, in a blank tone and without turning. "We'll have to make them spot us first. At night it's practically impossible to catch the Terrorists by surprise. Turn the lights on, and in the worst case scenario, fire only at my order."

Julia gripped the flashlight she wore on her hip, letting go of her rifle which now dangled from its shoulder strap. Skintilla had made it clear that the Terrorists were essentially nocturnal and disoriented by sudden and strong lights. With no permission to shoot if not in extreme circumstances, on a recon mission like that, the flashlight was the best weapon at Julia's disposal.

The Forest appeared deep and impenetrable, but finally in the forced silence of their march, they all could distinctly hear the noise of leaves rustled by something far more physical than the wind – those who followed Skintilla's eyes, like Julia, caught for a moment the source of the sound.

The Terrorists' sentinel stood on a branch in all his 2 meters of height, a spectral epiphany in the milky light of the moon. His long and fair hair stretched all the way to his waist, where his clothing started, a pair of rough britches sown with the skin of some animal... but the eyes, the eyes were really striking, wild and extremely bright, in that face otherwise so human.

The Instructor barely opens her lips, starts raising an arm to point to their silent observer - before the words take shape, a dull thud, quick minor rustling.

The Terrorist leaves the small group behind, runs down his path, slides through the bushes like an

**arrow in the air, shatters the silence of the Forest with
long, extended calls.**

"Over there -"

Skintilla's words, too late.

"Did he say attack or retreat?"

The question was an uncontrolled eruption from Julia's
lips, once the alarm had been given and no reason
remained for the rigid silence of their earlier march.

Skintilla shook her head and shrugged nervously.

"I don't know. We don't know their language."

"Shall we move on?"

The Instructor shot her a piercing look.

"No. We can't risk falling into an ambush."

The students tightened their circle, alert and wary, while
Skintilla raised her head slightly towards the leafy ceiling,
as if maximizing all her senses. The Forest was silent, and
at last she broke the silence, curt and peremptory.

"We'll have to make do with this sighting for today.
Retreat."

๛

"Do you think Skintilla is unsatisfied? Did we make a lot of mistakes the other night?"

"On the contrary. You were silent enough to approach a village sentinel as a first sighting."

Marcus' voice was calm and reassuring as usual.

"You had to retreat because you were performing a recon mission, not an attack - there would have been casualties in a battle."

Small wrinkles formed on Julia's forehead due to her thoughtful expression, and the Secretary was quick to catch it. With an uncommon and unexpected gesture he placed his hand on the girl's shoulder, gently forcing her to look at him in the eyes.

"Never underestimate your enemy. I know what you're thinking. How can they worry us, when we have flashlights and rifles and they have spears and arrows."

Marcus pointed to the sky and the sun with his free hand, without letting go of Julia's shoulder.

"By day, you're right, they're not a problem. That's why they hide. But at night... at night they act before us and more precisely. We don't wear plastiresin armor because it looks good. Skilled spears and arrows can kill before you even get a chance to open fire."

Julia could only nod in acknowledgement, somehow surprised by Marcus' intensity. He fell silent and let his hand fall back down. She decided to break the silence.

"I was thinking about something else as well."

The Secretary lifted his gaze and answered with his usual tone, light and curious.

"I'm listening."

"Skintilla said we don't know the Terrorists' language..."

"It's true."

"... and yet if we could translate it, we could prevent many of their operations."

"This is true, but they are usually not prone to conversation. The rare times we had a chance of capturing some individuals alive, they shut themselves in a stubborn silence and let themselves die."

The girl looked towards the green expanse of the Forest, beyond the walls.

"It's a pity. I would have liked to know that the Terrorist said, the other night."

Marcus hesitated before answering, his gaze momentarily distant.

"Perhaps you have given me an idea. I was thinking we could elaborate some kind of interpretation of their language studying statistics of cause/effect from recordings of their vocalizations."

Julia tilted her head, surprised by this speculation and by the reasoning the Secretary seemed to be carrying first of all with himself, and only secondarily with her.

"Interesting."

Marcus stopped talking to himself and smiled at her.

"I'll talk about it with the Knowledge Department of the Ministry."

~§~

The classroom was bright, with diagonal beams of sunlight cutting through the room, casting pools of liquid gold on the wooden floor. Skintilla was standing in front of the entire course, her hair shiny and similar to a flame sending out thousands of reflections. She spoke with a warm voice which carried a certain amount of unconcealed pride.

"We have returned without casualties from our first sighting in the Forest. This is a success, because it means we have acted with coordination and without mistakes."

Julia Dream

The Instructor wasn't the kind of person accustomed to wasting time in useless compliments - her appreciation gave way to shoulder patting and handshakes in the group, who received these words as sincere. While observing the group, Julia noticed that Marcus was watching carefully from a corner of the room – when their eyes met, he smiled and greeted her with a small saluting gesture.

Skintilla waited for the buzz created by her words to pass, before continuing her speech.

"We have studied together how to defend ourselves, with or without weapons; how to deal with the requests of our friends and the threats of our enemies. We have probed the depths of the Forest and discovered the power of music."

The Instructor allowed herself to endow her students with a satisfied smile.

"We may say all this has yielded its results."

Julia was listening carefully, her head relaxed and slightly tilted sideways. Thanks to her Ministry experience she knew well enough that the whole point of the speech had yet to come.

Skintilla artfully cleared her voice, in an implicit signal that underlined the following words, making them stand out among the others.

"In the following days you'll start a next phase of your training."

The joyful atmosphere became something close to sincere bewilderment, observed with interest by Marcus and Julia both from their respective positions: one was mentally registering the student's reaction to the news, the other slightly smiling at herself for having guessed in advance the logical conclusion of the speech.

Despite Skintilla's compliments, they weren't ready yet.

The group was pouring out of the classroom, which was becoming more and more silent with the gradual departure of buzzing comments to the Instructor's speech. Marcus' eyes followed Julia, who was keeping herself at the end of the line, listening to everyone and keeping her opinion to herself. He slowly reached her side, and she lagged behind in order to place a distance between her and the others.

"The ending of Skintilla's speech didn't surprise you, did it?"

Julia shook her head, ruffling her hair in doing so, and shrugged.

"Let's say that since I don't quite feel ready for the Advanced Corps yet, I didn't expect her to promote us, besides congratulating us."

Marcus thoughtfully nodded, sporting a half smile which somehow looked almost bitter.

"As for feeling ready, you probably never will until you experiment your role."

He adjusted his wording when he saw the girl's worried face, and smiled at her.

"For the rest, your reasoning is correct."

They walked down the central path of the base, and Julia shot a glance at the treetops of the Forest, as they swayed in the afternoon breeze. Marcus followed her eyes.

"We won't be holding our lesson today."

He briefly looked at the ground, before looking back at her.

"You are correct. I approached you because I wanted to say goodbye. I'm leaving."

Julia remained petrified, feeling abandoned and terribly foolish. She looked distant while listening to Marcus' words.

"You no longer have gaps to fill, in comparison to the others here. My presence is no longer necessary."

Student Mayne lowered her head and sketched a small curtsy.

"Goodbye then, and my sincere thanks for the time dedicated to me, Secretary."

He answered with his cheerful voice, resounding of controlled laughter, making her raise her eyes to meet his gaze.

"There is no need to return to formality, Julia. Nothing changes between us. I'm sure we'll meet again soon."

"Very well. See you soon, then. Goodbye Marcus."

She couldn't think of anything else to say, but she tried to smile. Then she shut herself in her room to think.

∽

She flopped on the bed, frustrated by her own sadness. She stared at the videophone for a while, fighting with her wish to call Cleo, but she only had one call left, and one communication so close to the other would only alarm her sister, and burn all possibility of contact for an indefinite amount of time.

Rolling on her side, she turned her back to the videophone, her feet still sticking out from the foot of the bed. She messily kicked away her boots, crawled her way upwards to place her head on the pillow, and curled up with her knees close to her chest.

Marcus' departure was a stinging ache, and she was now missing someone who could provide answers. Instructor Skintilla wasn't particularly keen on conversation and her classmates were still distant figures, even though they were no longer hostile. Furthermore, the Secretary's knowledge was difficult to equal in span and depth.

She rolled once again on the bed, finally noticing the chair next to the wardrobe where she usually piled her clothes, and the small object resting on a piece of paper.

Since I take it you like music, I decided to leave you some to study before our next chat on the matter.

You will find all kinds of melodies. From tracks good for relaxing, to those stimulating motivational centers or meditation. With the due nuances, of course.

Enjoy!

M.

Julia smiled while reading the card, then examined the gadget the Secretary had left for her. It looked similar to the remote control that had regulated the Ministry's hologram projector, but it was connected to a wire ending in two extremities she decided to interpret as earphones. She placed the soft plastiresin spheres in her ears and turned the device on. And then, she was no longer alone. She was embraced by a waterfall of notes, charmed in their spell for hours, staring at the ceiling and studying new worlds, in the flow of music.

∾

She got up at last to go to dinner, since her presence was required. The flat afternoon with no lessons had revealed itself an odd experience. She removed her earphones and delicately placed the music device on the chair next to the bed.

She brushed her fingertips on the precious instrument with a silent smile of thanks for Marcus, before pulling her boots on and exiting the room.

"Hey, Mayne!"

On her way out, she crossed Kob, who was probably heading to dining hall as well. They met in the corridor and he spoke to her confidentially, as they walked the distance together.

"Since you're always informed about things, do you happen to know when the new phase the Instructor was talking about is going to begin?"

Julia shook her head, truthfully.

"Unfortunately not. I know nothing more than what we were told earlier on."

Kob snorted.

"I hope it's going to start soon. I didn't know what to do this afternoon."

"I don't think they'll keep us waiting for a long time."

"You think so? I hope so."

"I do think so. It's not in the Empire's interest to slow down our training, if not for a reason."

"Do you see this reason?"

"Relax. I don't."

Julia Dream

∼◊

Later that night, in the private darkness of her room, hands crossed on her stomach – intent on elaborating nutrition from the recent meal – Julia found herself pondering on the conversation with Kob. A new phase was about to begin, and the absence of an important guide like Marcus was considerable.

She sighed and closed her eyelids, rolling around restlessly. Thoughts seemed to trip on the invading notes of that afternoon's music; fleeting and elusive, they refused to shut up or regularly flow in the memory of a consistent melody.

The girl placed her right arm on her forehead, as if the gesture could clear her thoughts.

IV

She flies on the floor, pushed by invasive hands, a sudden intense light shatters her eyelids. Face on the ground, she slams knees and elbows, attempts to turn, but then the first blows arrive - kicks, strong, on the floating ribs. Breathing is broken and she doubles up, curls, tucks her head in her knees and shoulders seeking to avoid the blows raining in from all sides.
"What did I do? What did I do? WhatDidIDo?"
Panic explodes vocally in a thought expressed without conscience or control, but instead of answers, more blows and hands, hands that in between one blow and another force the shoulders open, block trembling wrists around her back, yank her head back by her hair and force the new darkness of a black hood on her eyes.

Unable to move and defenseless, Julia relaxed without further resistance. She tried to breathe regularly and calm her racing heart, while a solid grip on her arms dragged her away. After seconds she was thrown to the ground, in a corner probably, since she had slammed her head on two sides. From the vibrations of the environment she guessed she was moving.

Trying to ignore the pain, shock and fear, she released all of her muscles trying to control their shaking, forcing her mind to work.

Voices closing in interrupted the slow, confused but constant stream of her thoughts.

"Looks like she fainted."

"Follow the procedure."

An increase in the vibrations of the floor warned Julia of approaching footsteps, and she found herself shivering subconsciously, trying to curl into a ball. She was startled by a cold hand grasping the back of her neck – she could feel herself invested by a wave of fear, then a small sting.

৶

"Do you know why you're here?"

The harsh voice shattered the darkness of unconsciousness. Behind her, the smell of damp earth, recent rain. She winced, struck by a gray artificial light, eyes blinking and teary when they removed the suffocating and stuffy darkness of the hood. She barely acknowledged the question, following with her gaze the two men which were flanking her, before taking position in front of the door she had just crossed.

The figure that had spoken was sitting at a desk, composed, impersonal, a talking uniform with a blank voice.

"Do you know what you have done?"

Julia remained motionless in the empty hall, shrugging and crossing her arms, realizing she was cold, a cold that made her limbs shake, her hands rigid - a cold paralyzing her in the inappropriateness of her thin frayed shirt.

The calm in the face and voice of the officer at the desk was thinning, and he went up to the girl, inspecting her contemptuously.

"Shall I add insubordination to the list of your charges? I demand answers. Do you know or imagine why you are here?"

Julia stared at the ground. Words were having a hard time coming out.

"I... I didn't do anything."

The officer shot her a penetrating look, then started circling around her, hands crossed behind his back, his voice once again blank.

"Nothing? So why do you think you are here then?"

For the long moment while she stared in the eyes of her interlocutor, looking at him from down to up, Julia was once again the Champion of the Empire, winner on the field against the professional Maxim. Cold and sharp as a blade, her eyes carved in ice.

"I believe my presence here to be part of my training."

She raised her head, tilting it slightly backwards in a rush of pride.

The officer placed a hand on her shoulder and unexpectedly smiled.

"Correct. And look..."

He indicated the door behind Julia, which opened on a courtyard marked by a handful of wooden huts. It was embraced by a palisade, and sported a conspicuous gate protected by two guards.

"The door is open. You can leave this place whenever you want, and give up on your training."

The girl turned around, following the movement of the hand on her shoulder, guiding her to contemplate that sight. She squinted because of the glare of the natural light and tensed her muscles, expecting a trap or an imminent blow, but nothing happened.

Only a light pat on the back.

"If you decide to stay, just know it's not going to be easy. Few resist."

~δ

A drop of water fell on the naked skin of her shoulder, waking her. She opened her eyes and grimaced because of the pain coursing in her limbs, cluttered with bruises following the entire color scale of injuries, from violet to greenish yellow.

She curled up with her knees close to her breast to compensate the shiver of cold which followed, but soon another drop fell on her arm. She raised her eyes to the ceiling - it was raining in the hut once again.

She sat up from the dust bed she had prepared in the driest corner she could find, doubling up almost immediately because of a deep, chesty cough. The dryness in her throat and the weight on her forehead suggested a fever. Standing up uncertainly, propping herself with one hand on the wall of the hut to balance the weakness in her legs, she ventured out in the open with a couple of unsteady steps.

The clouds which were gathering were a glaring light gray which hurt her eyes, and the drops falling out of the sky were still rare, even if huge.

Julia tilted her head backwards and opened her mouth, oblivious to the quality of the water, interested only in quenching her thirst. The first day after her arrival she had waited for a ration of something - water, food, pills, anything - but there had been nothing. The second day she had decided she was going to make do with the rain.

Two or three drops fell on her parched tongue and lips: she would have cried in frustration, had she held enough liquids in her body to produce tears. Then her eyes fell on a puddle nearby. She strode over to it with a determination that for a moment made her shine with dignity, there under the bored derision of the camp guards.

She let herself fall on her knees at the border of the small muddy hollow, and would have lapped up the water like a dog in absence of a better idea. She sank her hands just below the surface, trying to filter the mud and let at least some of the dirt deposit.

She remained there as long as it was necessary, kneeling, drinking one sip of dirty water at a time - she stopped only when she started feeling a movement and an increasing pain in her digestive system, violently awakened. She passed her tongue on her gums, trying to clean the dust out of the sores that had come out where she had cut her inner cheek with her teeth.

She closed her eyes for a second, banishing any motion of self-pity as utterly useless. When she opened them again, she fixed her determined gaze on the muddy soil. She would use it later on to fix the water infiltrations in the hut.

∾

Light, white and cold; it breaks the damp semi-darkness of the room. She curls up but no blows arrive - hands pick her up, lift her to her feet, push her out. She trips in the mud but does not fall, held back.

The lighting beacons hurt the eyes, confused footsteps in the barracks' rooms, as Julia is pushed face-forward

on a bright white wall - the palm of her hands breaks the fall, not without repercussions the muscles of neck and shoulders.

"Stay here. Don't try to move."

The snarl of an unidentified voice.

Julia falls to her knees, is about to turn around, hands grab her and pull her up again.

"Stay still and don't move!"

Hands resting on the wall, she blinks in the painful glare, closes reddened eyes, and her head falls forward, forehead on the wall.

1, 2, 3 seconds of peace. A yank in her hair, her face against the wall, another yank.

"Stand up and don't sleep!"

Julia started counting. The 9 times table, keeping her mind active to forget the uncontrollable shaking of her legs, the cough, the pain, the distance from any affection, serenity or peace.

"This is what you want, right?"

Cleo's voice emerging from the abyss of distance in space and time, clear and remote in memory.

"I thought I wanted it, I don't know anymore" Julia argued in tears, at number count 11727.

The undecipherable voice of the Secretary, that distant day in his study.

"You'll have time to thank me."

Marcus knew, he knew what they would put her through! The meticulous chain of numbers in Julia's mind was interrupted by an explosion of anger and she could feel a wave of despair overwhelming her - even though she had no tears left, her trembling increased, no longer kept at bay by mindful reasoning.

She slumped to the ground, senseless.

She was woken up by a circular, constant sound; a siren. She was once again in the wooden shack. She crawled for a few inches to look out of the hut without having to stand up, an action far beyond her forces.

Beyond the invasive noise, there was nothing unusual in the camp - the guards at the gate had a bored look on their faces, while other pale, spectral figures like her dragged themselves out to lick some muddy water. She noticed for the first time that there were other prisoners in the structure, but this vision didn't alleviate her solitude or fatigue in any way.

The siren stopped, abruptly as it had started. Julia relaxed the muscles of her shoulders which were keeping her perched at the door, falling heavily with torso and head on the floor. She shut her eyes, yearning for the peace of sleep.

Already her mind was travelling on dreamy paths, when a high-pitched and insisting whistle pierced her thoughts - she woke up, falling in a state of tired awakening, but the whistle did not leave.

Recruit Mayne clenched her fists and rested her forehead on the floor: this new, jarring noise was coming from the same loudspeakers that had been broadcasting the sound of the siren earlier on.

Painfully, Julia curled up with her knees to her breast and covered her ears with her hands, clenching her elbows - at first she didn't even notice the tears of frustration that were inexorably rolling down her cheeks. Feeling the dampness slide down from her face to her forearm and wrist, she bit her lip until she could taste the blood.

Julia Dream

The call ended. She slowly took her hands away from her ears, unsure in the new-found silence. It was merely three seconds, before the whistle started again, loud and teasing. Julia quit the idea of sleep, and turned the sound in a spindle for spinning her hate.

∽

The noises, different and prolonged, lasted for two days and two nights. When at last the cry of the loudspeakers provided a truce, Julia slept an anxious and irregular sleep. Her eyes would snap open after brief intervals, expecting the hateful siren, only to heavily drop for the deep fatigue. Before cold and fever claimed her consciousness, she wondered what else were they going to take from her.

She would stare at the open gate of the camp, an exit to the dense green surrounding the structure. For a long time she looked at the dirt path that led from the opening down into the Forest.

She could leave all that pain behind. But to go where? To a humiliating return to the Ministry? To head out alone and unarmed in Terrorist territory, in her condition? Or perhaps was it a quick firing squad that awaited those who were foolish enough to trust their jailors? The open door inflicted the acute torment of choice - fear of future pain clashed with the terror of the wrong decision.

From time to time Julia would rest her forehead on the floor, trying to distract her eyes and attention from the fixed thought of the gate, from the whirling conjectures of her tired mind. Her will to resist, to pursue her goal, was eroded by doubt - that the right answer could be the simplicity of escaping from such a terrible place.

But it was in the nature of soldier Mayne to be inclined towards persistence, stubbornness and suspicion, rather than opportunism - in her mind, anyone could leave the structure, without necessary calculating the risk, and very few would remain... so to pass the test she would have to stay. A desperate and recurring analysis.

She mustered all her will to force herself to stand up and take a few steps, to fight the pain in her muscles and the whirl of her thoughts.

The slow, yet constant, steps betray her – lead her to the gate, where Julia notices one of the guards for the first time, not only a blank voice or a heavy hand, but

a person, an obvious individuality. A young man, deep and warm black eyes, uncontaminated by indifference.

Words slip out of chapped lips.

"I can't stand it any longer. I'm dying."

And then an answer resonates in the air, before the unconscious truth makes its way in a muddy, miserable conscience, cuts the silence like the hint of a secret smile.

"Don't worry. It's almost over."

Julia felt stunned as she returned to the hut, spending her last energies trying to make sense of the bizarre conversation. Those words and their elusive subject floated in her brain, almost reduced to mere sounds in the ebb of her feverish thoughts.

For even if the basic question was disquieting – *what* was almost over? – she could no longer worry about the answer. Because music had arrived.

Sequences of notes, heard by chance or casually, melodies coming from training with Skintilla, enriched in her mind with new and ephemeral harmonies. Music burst in, unexpected and inescapable like destiny, de-structuring

Julia Dream

every form of reasoning in feverish delirium, all consistent
thought in elegant series of notes.

V

The first strange detail to float at the border of her consciousness was that she did not feel cold. Initially she felt a slight and diffused warmth, then a light weight on her back, and a sinking feeling on a soft surface.

"I believe she is waking up."

The familiar voice shook sleep off her, as she connected the dots in her mind. Marcus. The sudden contraction of her stomach, followed by the warm sting of acid up her esophagus, sent its metallic aftertaste all the way to her clenched teeth. She breathed out slowly, relaxing her jaw and opening her eyes. She was struck by the whiteness of the pillowcase of her soft headrest, of the blanket that covered her.

She painfully turned in the direction of the voice, fixing a firm glare on Marcus, who answered by lowering his head in an obvious admission of guilt, as the doctor with whom the Secretary had been talking hurried out of the room without a word.

At that point Julia let her head fall back down on the pillow, and spoke staring at the ceiling.

"And now, what are you going to do to me?"

Marcus looked up and shook his head, attempting a small smile.

"Nothing. Your training is over. You're only missing your nomination."

She stared at him coldly.

"You were right, had I known I would not have thanked you."

"I can understand that."

Still not looking at him in the eye, the girl arched her back, stretching the muscles of her shoulders and arms as to test them. She spoke in an absent tone that betrayed emotions she could barely contain.

"Sometimes I feared the test was to simply be smart enough to leave. What did you do to those who left the camp?"

The Secretary tilted his head slightly while answering her, as if surprised by the question.

"Nothing. The camp is just a few kilometers away from the base. They will be able to keep on working here in an intermediate position between their old rank and the Advanced Corps."

"Oh."

He noticed she had gone white, and then had blushed.

"Why do you ask?"

The girl looked away, her eyes clouded at the memory of recent pain.

"I feared you would unceremoniously execute those who abandoned the camp, as a punishment for their failure."

For the first time since she had known him, Marcus stared at her speechless, truthfully appalled - when at last he found his voice, his tone made it clear the Secretary was truly scandalized.

"I will have to engage in a little talk with Yrenes."

"Why?"

"Because her superficial and trivial ways have done incalculable damage."

Julia could feel tears starting to burn behind her eyes and in her throat, in the face of the exemplary yet incomplete truth of this statement. The Secretary kept on pouring salt in the wound.

"Do you remember why the Empire was created in the first place?"

"To unite, reorganize and save the human race."

Marcus nodded.

"And what did humanity do for the Empire?"

"It abandoned its superstitions and gods, because they had led only to folly and nonsense. It wasn't a god that saved our ancestors, but the idea they created for themselves of an Empire that could reunite them."

Marcus nodded again.

"Exactly. At least they did teach you this. You really think the Empire would put down precious human resources only because they don't show exceptional skills?"

The hatred in Julia's eyes dampened into a cautious and very tired look.

"I guess not."

Marcus was forced to accept that, and even as he smiled at her, he was obviously worried.

"Good. Remember that."

The Secretary looked at her straight in the eye.

"What you had to bear was harsh, but there are worse things."

Julia suppressed a snarl, and nodded ironically.

"So I suppose I should thank you for what you didn't do to me?"

Marcus shook his head.

"I'm not asking you to be thankful, but to think about it."

The only answer was a sullen silence, and the Secretary sighed.

"I've brought some clothes here for you. Is there anything you need?"

Julia nodded, sitting up on the bed.

"Yes. A shower."

ᕬ

Eyes pierce the steam and land on the mirror - hard as shards of iron, puzzling like a frozen abyss. Julia observes her own body, bright eyes in a frighteningly pale face following the darting muscles under the skin of arms, torso, back. The greenish, yellow remains of bruises, cuts and scabs that still have to heal.

She keeps on looking until the steam veils the mirror and the hate in her stare.

ᕬ

"Julia!"

Cleo's smile quickly faded, as she observed her sister. The joy on her face instantly turned into a surprised and worried frown.

"What did they do to you?"

Julia brought thin fingers to her face, touching her cheekbones with her fingertips, exhibiting a small nervous smile.

"Have I lost much weight?"

Cleo looked at her sternly, snapping nervously - she knew her sister too well to be fooled like that.

"It's not that. It's all the rest that has changed."

Soldier Mayne was surprised by the strength of that statement, and her composure softened as she gave in to curiosity.

"What has changed, Cleo?"

The younger girl's smile shone again for a moment.

"Nothing between us."

She kept on speaking, seriously, before Julia could change the subject.

"But your aura, your eyes, your way of occupying space have completely changed."

"In what sense?"

"As if you had metal in your veins, not blood, and had received so much hammering on the forge that you have become a weapon. Should you meet Maxim today, you would slaughter him and continue on your way without even glancing at him twice. They have turned all your fears in hate and rage."

Julia bowed her heady, her eyes veiled by a sudden sadness at the truth of those words. When she spoke her voice was tired and wavering.

"I don't even know if this is what they wanted."

Cleo's voice piped back up as she realized how much her sister's mood had darkened.

"What they wanted is not important. It seems obvious you need some rest. When are you coming home?"

Julia lifted her eyes and smiled.

"I should be there in two days."

≈

Champion of the Empire Mayne received the rank of Advanced Corps Captain on a cold and rainy day of the eleventh month. She was alone at the ceremony, nor did she receive any information on her comrades. She didn't ask.

Her eyes were following the raindrops on the other side of the window pane, as Skintilla read the oath of loyalty to the Emperor out loud.

"I vow, in the name of the memory of the Cataclysm, to follow with loyalty the figure who guided us in that moment, and all those who act in his name."

Julia's voice sounded terribly young, as she pronounced those solemn words in a perfectly inexpressive tone.

"I confirm my commitment to dedicating my life and actions to the survival of the human race and the common good."

When the ceremony was over, Julia finally tore her gaze away from the rain to look at Skintilla - the Instructor nodded and Marcus signed the papers as witness.

There was no storm that day in the eyes of the newly promoted Captain. Her irises were dark pools of deep and cold desolation, for Julia could feel, like claws in her guts, that this apparent success had been paid for with a life of sacrifice and pain that could not be compensated by a pat on the back and gold paint on her cage. She was aware she was just a number in the mechanism of the Empire, a number where she had merely gained a digit.

Skintilla solemnly handed over a copy of her new identification badge, and informed her that new uniforms for her stay in the city had already been delivered to her room. She opened and shut her right fist, mechanically accepting the object from the Instructor, who sent her an encouraging smile, before leaving the room with a formal salute and a flash of her hair.

Julia found herself face to face with Marcus. To her surprise, he was also handing her something.

"Take it. It's yours."

His dark eyes looked at the impassible face of the young Captain, and she found herself looking at her left hand, where the Secretary had slipped a small metal object.

The girl closed her fingers on the music reader Marcus had left her before leaving. Trying to ignore the chaos she was feeling in her chest, she raised her gaze to look at her mentor. She twisted her lips in the attempt of a smile.

"Thank you."

᜶

Julia sits at the side of the bed in a room that soon won't be hers, stares at the wall with the dull display of the videophone, her hands on the covers, knuckles just barely raised and nails scratching at the soft surface of the mattress.

She closes her eyes for a moment, then her back arches forwards and her entire figure shrivels up, forehead resting on her knees. From the shaking of her shoulders, and suffocated moans, it is clear that Captain Mayne is crying, crying for hours.

VI

The door opened up, recognizing Cleo's badge. Blonde curls wavered for a moment when the girl was startled by the figure rising to meet her from the sofa – a second later she was jumping in her sister's arms, who was so surprised she hesitated a moment before squeezing her tightly, a smile of sheer delight on her face.

"Cleo! How are you?"

The girl look at Julia in the eye, happy to see the light burning in there and beaming a smile in return.

"I'm fine. Did you have a good trip?"

The aerovehicle abandons the deserted base in the deep dark preceding dawn, and from the window a swath of dense ink briefly turns to red, revealing a landscape of clouds which soon become homogeneously gray.

Her head leaning on a side, tired half-closed eyes, Julia ponders, her stare as gray as the scenery and the thick silence dividing her from Marcus.

Julia Dream

"... I guess not, from the face you made."

Cleo's eyebrows arched in a worried expression, but Julia shook her head to flick off the memories, and smiled at her.

"Don't worry, no problem. What about you?"

She looked at her sister, weighing her minute features, her thin wrists.

"You've lost weight."

Cleo was quick to react.

"Look who's talking!"

"My diet has been variable, yours is stable."

"I was nervous and didn't sleep much, lately."

She lowered her eyes, as if ashamed to speak of her own health. Julia noticed and smiled at her once again.

"I didn't mean to embarrass you, I just want to make sure you are ok."

Cleo lifted her eyes and smiled back.

"I'm fine, I'm fine."

"So, what about this Dreas?"

"He said he was going to leave us alone so we could talk freely."

"I understand. But I'm curious."

Cleo grinned, not without some malice.

"I think he's quite afraid of the Champion of the Empire."

Julia's shoulders flopped down to a sad position.

"Oh come on, what did you tell him?"

Cleo's expression returned serious.

"Nothing, he found out we were related when I didn't show up at the Study Center the days before the duel."

Julia nodded.

"I see."

Cleo's tone lightened once again.

"Anyway, I see your uniform is different, but I don't know what that means. Tell me everything!"

"Oh."

Julia's voice was blanker than she would have wished.

"They promoted me to the Advanced Corps with the rank of Captain."

"You don't seem very happy about it."

"I'm afraid I don't know in what mess I've just landed."

For a moment it seemed that Cleo was going to say something, but she didn't, with a face that was not lost to her sister.

"What were you going to say?"

Julia's peremptory tone made Cleo jump, and she shrugged guiltily and shook her head.

Julia Dream

"I was thinking that you could always turn back if you wanted to, but then I realized that obviously after all the sacrifices you made, you have no intention doing anything like that. It was a stupid thought, sorry."

At these words the Captain felt her shoulders slump from the weight of great sense of fatigue, and flopped down on the couch, bringing a hand to her forehead.

"No, you should excuse me. It's that you're right, I wouldn't stand turning back, not after…"

She stopped mid-sentence, but it was too late.

Cleo sat by her side, taking her shoulder and turning her around to look at her in the eye.

Her voice, dense with worry, demanded an answer.

"Julia, what did they do to you?"

❧

Cleo was lying on the bed, glancing sideways towards Julia, who had fallen asleep immediately, showing just how much rest she still required to return to complete health. The girls had spoken of the training in the R3 base, but unsaid words were still lingering in the air, suffocated by a dark fear and a strange sense of shame.

Julia Dream

Captain Mayne was sleeping entirely curled up, in a position Cleo had not seen her sleep in for years, since before her work at the Ministry. Suddenly, she started shaking - thinking she might be cold, Cleo got up to fetch another blanket, but a reflection of the dim light revealed tears streaking down Julia's cheeks in her restless sleep.

Cleo clenched her fists and bit her lip, crestfallen, uncertain, and in that moment Julia turned and opened her eyes, upset and tired but clearly awake. She closed her eyes once again and whispered sleepily.

"You can't sleep? Am I bothering you?"

"No, no. It's not you."

"I'm sorry. Dreas could have stayed, I would have slept on the couch."

Cleo sat up quickly, underlining her word with the gesture.

"Are you kidding? I'm happy to be with you, and I often ask Dreas to sleep at his own house anyway."

Julia kept her eyes closed, but frowned in the dark.

"Why?"

"I don't want the Office for Resource Management to open a procedure to reassign this house, with the excuse that you are out and Dreas and I share a bed."

Julia opened her eyes and took Cleo's hand, squeezing it gently for a moment.

"They won't. It's part of my deal with Marcus, that and the Level I Education Permit."

Cleo squeezed her hand in return, scowling.

"Are you sure the price you're paying for all of this isn't too high? We can try other ways."

Julia smiled slightly, shaking her head from the pillow, eyes closing once again under the power of an intrusive sleep.

"No, don't worry. I could never return to the Ministry."

And then she fell asleep.

∽

When the buzz of the alarm echoed in the half-shadow of the room, Cleo noticed that Julia was already up. She pulled a jacket on and went out to look for her sister.

She found her on the floor of the entrance hall of the house, intent in doing push-ups.

34, 35, 36. The right arm gives up at the thirty seventh push-up, Julia ends up sprawled on the cold tiled floor.

She stubbornly lowers her head, oblivious to Cleo's perplexed look, and performs the last three elements of the series slowly, arms trembling. She stands up without raising her eyes, zips up the coat of her black city uniform, wiping the sweat from her forehead with her hand.

"Good morning!"

Julia jumped, turning around and seeing Cleo.

"Hello! I hadn't noticed you."

"You're doing your homework?"

A smile softened Cleo's ironic expression, while the Captain slowly sat down on the sofa, crossing her arms as if cold.

"No, I don't feel fit. I had to stop because of cold sweat."

"You have to leave tomorrow for your new assignment?"

Julia nodded, turning around to rummage in one of her backpacks, still talking.

"Yes. I have an appointment with Marcus today to understand what the mission is about."

She pulled out of the bag a yellow object, a little longer than her hand and slightly bent inwards.

"I'm sure you'll be fine."

Julia Dream

Julia raised her eyes to look at Cleo and smiled, her eyes not gray but light blue and shining in her pale face.

"I hope so."

She pulled out a knife from a pocket, and opened it to reveal its 5-6 cm blade. Cleo watched her sister with fascination and surprise as she used the weapon to notch the outer layer of the yellow object to extract its content, seemingly soft, opaque and of a paler shade of yellow.

Rising to throw away the casing in the incinerator of the building, Julia tilted the object in Cleo's direction.

"Do you want to taste it? It's a banana, they say it's a very nourishing fruit."

She smiled, catching her sister's hesitation.

"It shouldn't bother you if you only take a small bite."

Cleo blinked cautiously, but finally surrendered to curiosity.

"Ok, I'll give it a try."

She took the tiny slice of the fruit between her thumb and index finger, placed it in her mouth and gulped it down, head back, like she would do with her tablets - a moment later she was coughing and trying to swallow.

Julia couldn't help laughing, while quickly grabbing a bottle of water from her bag and passing it to her sister.

"Not like that, you have to chew!"

"I think I understood that!"

Cleo's voice was still kind of strangled by the cough, but her eyes were shining. The joint laughter of the two sisters warmed the room.

≪

Nothing had changed in Marcus' elegant office - only the music was different, a kind of regular, rolling and powerful thunder.

The Secretary anticipated her question.

"It's the sound of the sea. I'll send it to you, if you like it."

He smiled, looking at her carefully with his dark brown eyes.

"You look well."

Julia couldn't hide a flash in her gray eyes; Marcus' smile broadened.

"Go ahead, I'm listening."

The girl shook her head, staring at the ground.

"I don't understand how you can say that. I couldn't do 40 push-ups without feeling sick this morning! I can't imagine what Skintilla would say."

Julia Dream

"She would say they are not necessary."

Julia remained in silence, enraged by the unclear joy on the Secretary's face, who completely ignored her words.

"Let me quickly go through your mission: I have the impression you might be interested."

She breathed out, hiding her fear behind a blank look, concentrating on Marcus' words.

"I spoke with the Department of Knowledge about your idea of translating the Terrorists' language."

Julia straightened up on the chair.

"They agree with me that such knowledge would be a great progress for us, compared to the current situation."

The Secretary paused again, conveying with this simple gesture the idea of long conversations and negotiation, his commitment and his effort in this project.

"The Department and I have also arrived to the conclusion that we can launch a research expedition. And this is where you come in the picture."

Julia was perfectly still, listening, her eyes half-closed.

"You have to gather a sample of the sounds the Terrorists make, as a reaction to different situations. You will have under your command about a dozen soldiers from Operational Base 07."

The girl recovered her speaking skills.

"But how am I supposed to guide them, if I can't even do a few push-ups!"

He observed her with his unflappable little smile.

"Captain Mayne, remember you are going to guide your troops with the agility of your mind, not with the strength of your arm."

Then he lowered his voice, softening his tone.

"Julia, I can understand your fear, but you'll see it's going to be fine. After all, this mission exists because of your idea."

Then Marcus recovered his usual professional tone, seeing that the girl was sighing, but had also relaxed a little.

"Questions?"

"Yes. Why was OB07 chosen?"

The Secretary nodded, as if approving the question.

"According to our data on the migration patterns of the Terrorists, more groups should soon converge in that area. Samples coming from different sources should help us understand if there are differences in the languages of the different groups."

"So, if I take this correctly, the quadrant is going to be densely populated - but I have to avoid a clash and merely provide the Terrorists with different situations which will allow me to record their sounds."

"Exactly."

"Is the aim of my mission going to be public? What am I supposed to tell my team?"

Marcus pulled a face, thoughtful.

"Formally, you don't even owe an explanation to the Commander of the base. I have already spoken with her personally."

He seemed to reflect a moment before speaking again.

"Probably the best course of action could be to maintain some privacy, without secrecy. How much you want to reveal is going to be your choice."

Julia pressed her lips together in a concentrated expression.

"Good."

"The aerovehicle will be waiting for you tomorrow at 17.00."

"Ok."

Marcus captured her gaze, looking at her intently.

"Keep me updated on your progress. I have provided you with a videophone with unlimited calls."

The Secretary winked, reading surprise and gratitude in the girl's gaping eyes – suddenly she appeared once again incredibly young. After a few seconds she found her voice, and addressed a shy smile in his direction.

"Thanks."

᠊᠊᠊᠊

"So, how did it go?"

"Could be worse. At least the mission comes from an idea of mine."

Cleo was leaning with her back to the window, her hands on the window sill behind her. Sitting on the couch, Julia was thoughtfully chewing on an apple.

"Basically I have to pick up material for a study on the Terrorists' language."

"You're not going out there to fight, then."

"No. That is not our objective for the moment."

Cleo breathed out, releasing some of her anxiety.

"Good."

She frowned.

"*Our* objective?"

"It appears that I'm going to be assigned a team of about ten units."

While saying these words, Julia had remained bowed down on her apple. The position of her shoulders, bent from the invisible weight of responsibility, betrayed her insecurity and so did her tone, where self-irony attempted to mask her fear.

Cleo smiled at her sister, even if she wasn't watching.

"I'm sure you'll find yourself at ease after a little while. From what you tell me, Marcus looks like the kind of person that knows what he's doing."

Julia looked slightly up, weighing these words.

"Yes... I guess. I'll get by."

She answered Cleo's smile.

"What about you? How did it go?"

"With what?"

"With the banana! Did you digest it without consequence?"

Cleo giggled.

"I think. I felt some strange movement, but no pain."

"Good. Do you want some of this apple?"

Julia Dream

Julia cut a piece of the fruit and stretched her arm out towards the sister, offering her a greenish slice - once again Cleo looked at it suspiciously.

"And what if I like it?"

Julia paused before answering, not because of hesitation but reflection. Her words resonated simple and determined.

"I will renegotiate my agreement with Marcus."

Cleo pulled back, shaking her head.

"Julia, no. I'm already a weight."

Her sister stared at her.

"Are you kidding? I've never considered you a weight!"

Cleo looked down, hiding her wet eyes with her curls.

"I don't want you to face further risks, especially not for me."

"Hey."

Julia spoke with unusual softness, forcing the younger girl to look at her with her calm gaze.

"Let's not worry too much before it's time – you might not even like the apple!"

Cleo sketched a smile.

"And then, I can always ask a favor from the Empire."

Her eyes darkened as she lowered her voice.

Julia Dream

"I don't feel much in debt anymore."

Cleo's frightened look softened her voice.

"Come on, just try this for the moment."

Hesitating, Cleo took the slice from Julia's hands and gingerly licked the coarse surface of the fruit, daring then a little nibble with her front teeth. She squeezed her eyes and pulled a face, chewing awkwardly.

"But it's..."

"Sour, I know."

Julia had learned the word from Marcus - Cleo barely registered the information, taken as she was by giving the nibbled slice back to her sister, laughing.

"I would say that for the moment I really don't feel the need to switch to a biological alimentation."

Julia smiled at this rapid mood change.

"All right. If you change your mind I'll have you taste other things, but perhaps for the moment it's better this way.

She unconsciously placed a hand on her stomach.

"Re-adjusting our digestive system is a pain."

Cleo smiled, but was soon serious again, her eyes the color of the Forest in autumn.

"Marcus didn't say how long you'll be away?"

Captain Mayne shook her head, sending ripples to her ponytail.

"No, but he did assign me a videophone with unlimited calls."

"Really? This makes me believe it's going to be a long mission, if he wants you to update him regularly."

"Or short – and the number of potential calls is limited."

Cleo nodded.

"This is also true... and I imagine much is going to depend on the material you can gather."

In the following silence, Julia stood up to throw the apple's core in the incinerator. She was not facing Cleo, when she was almost imperiously hailed by her sister.

She turned to meet her intense look.

"Julia? Promise me you're not going to take any unnecessary risks, to hurry?"

Captain Mayne froze, nailed down by this request, struck by how naturally Cleo had anticipated her thoughts and future temptation.

She nodded.

"I promise."

She then nodded again to herself, with a dry smile.

Julia Dream

"I'm starting to understand why Marcus wants to have me accompanied by a team."

VII

The weight of the armor was familiar and even comforting, as if the protective gear could hide and protect Julia, enclosed in the role of Captain Mayne: imperial moons engraved in the plastiresin of her protective collar illustrated her rank.

She had been assigned a spacious and comfortable habitation module, integrated in the dorms, but the portable videophone Marcus had granted her was the real luxury. For her mission the Secretary had provided her with recording equipment, torches and flash grenades. The Advanced Corps rifle Kalashnikov Beta was propped, along with other munitions, against the closet for her armor.

For other kinds of weapons Julia would have to depend on the arsenal of the base - for this reason her first priority was to create a feeling of mutual cooperation with Commander Nah, who was in charge of the outpost. Just like the Commander had no authority on a member of the Advanced Corps, similarly Julia held no rights on the structure.

The Commander's behavior to that moment justified high hopes. Upon her arrival the day earlier, Julia had been invited to rest from her long aerovehicle journey, in an accommodation that was far from modest. Now Captain Mayne was preparing to meet the Commander of the base for breakfast, in response to an invitation which promised a cordial approach to the cooperation imposed on them by the heads of the Ministry.

Upon her exit from the module, Julia was impressed by the efficiency of the cooling system of her accommodation, since directly from the door she impacted with what felt like a solid wall of heat and humidity. She swatted off a fly as big as her thumbnail with an annoyed gesture of her hand.

The Northern American jungle was quite different from the Forest she had experienced before. The outpost itself, clearly a temporary base, looked wilder than any imperial settlement she had ever seen - even the walls, despite the considerable size of the structure, were shrunk down to a high tension fence, propped up by the vigilance and attention of the technicians who were supervising the condition of the solar panels providing energy to the base.

Julia Dream

Captain Nah's tent was placed at the center and dominated the entire fenced area with its three floors. Hurrying to limit the time of exposure to the intense heat, and already beading with sweat, Julia headed decisively towards the odd building, where two men were guarding the entrance. They quickly saluted her, looking at her with curiosity, inviting her to take the stairs to the second floor, where the Commander was waiting for her.

The girl quickly climbed the metal spiral of the stairs, noting that she would have to talk with Cleo about this tent, sure that she would be interested: Cleo was directing her studies towards architecture, and Nah's tent was indeed a considerable example of ingenuity.

When Julia passed the curve described by the spiral just before reaching the floor, she found Commander Nah standing nearby, waiting for her. She was a beautiful woman in her thirties, tall and slim. Short and very light hair framed a face lit up by elegantly slanted green eyes. Even her voice had an exotic timbre, low and warm.

"Welcome to OB07, Captain."

"My thanks, Commander."

Julia responded with cautious courtesy, trying to weigh down how much her young age risked to undermine her position, potentially already uncomfortable.

Nah turned around slightly, to point at a sumptuously decked table that had been set for two.

"Come, let's sit. I hope you had a comfortable journey?"

She had sat down while speaking, and was pouring into their glasses an orange liquid from a pitcher placed at the center of the table. She emptied her drink in three or four sips.

"Yes, there were no storms on our way. I sincerely wish to thank you for your hospitality, I truly couldn't wish for a better accommodation."

Julia also sat down, observing carefully the environment and the Commander. All the second floor of the tent was occupied by that single room: the table, laden with steel trays of sliced and peeled fruit, was placed next to the stairs taking down to the ground floor, while on the other side of the hall, towards the stairs going up, the Commander had set a steel desk and a couple of chairs.

"I'm glad you find your quarters appropriate."

Nah looked at Julia's empty plate and full glass and smiled.

"You may eat and drink as you please. That is the juice of our oranges, while over there we have mango, and banana. All local production, they grow naturally in the Forest."

Julia smiled back, taking the glass to her lips and carefully sipping the orange liquid. She was surprised by the taste at first, sour and sweet at the same time, but soon understood that the intense heat made the juice the perfect drink for the climate. She lingered a moment with the cup in her hand, gathering ideas and courage. The pleasantries were not going to last much longer.

The Commander spoke again, looking for Julia's eyes from above the glass.

"Secretary Marcus has asked me to provide you with a dozen of my units. I could help you in your choice if you would like to share with me further information on your mission. Currently we only have half of our forces in the base, but I can nonetheless offer you a rose of about 600 candidates."

Julia's eyes met the intense green of Nah's stare. The Commander was sure of what she was doing and had no fear of an inspection – she deserved an answer.

Captain Mayne nodded slightly.

"Thank you. My mission is part of a recent project of the Department of Knowledge. I have to gather information on the Terrorists."

Julia paused and Nah leaned forward on the table, interested.

"I was sent here because the Ministry has acknowledged different groups of Terrorists converging in this area."

The Commander nodded, relaxing her back and stretching her long legs under the table.

"So they are. Half of my troops are deployed 20km from here to prevent our enemy from getting too close. For the moment they are coming from North and East – the Ocean protects us from the West, and OB08 is not encountering issues on the South."

"I need someone that can watch my back."

"If you don't need the specific skills of bomb disposal experts or scouts, I suggest you consider our recruits. Some of them are in excellent shape. You could watch them while they train, if you want."

"Thank you for the offer. I was planning on scouting the border, on our side of the Forest, to become familiar with the environment. After that I'll gladly follow the activities of the base, to understand where I can find the best subjects for this mission."

Nah nodded approvingly.

"Good. I can have someone give you a ride on an electrocart, we have trails we use to supply our units in the front lines. I'll make sure your driver will be ready when you want to leave."

Julia nodded her thanks, accepting this final courtesy of the Commander.

"Thank you. I'll be ready soon."

◆

The pilot's name was Arl, and he was the Sub-Commander Nah had nominated for the base. Julia noted the Commander's ability to keep an eye on her guests without formally disrespecting them, but wasn't upset about it.

The Sub-Commander knew the area well and was driving with ease and confidence. He appeared to be a few years younger than Nah, and had probably spent great part of his training and career in base 07.

After little more than half an hour, Julia asked him to stop about 5km away from the border.

"I'm going to familiarize with the territory. I'll be back in two hours at most."

The girl jumped off the vehicle, which was silently hovering about half a meter from the ground of the dirt trail, propped against its rear brake. Just before closing the door, following a whim of the moment, she grabbed a cylindrical object from one of the electrocart's front compartments.

"I'm taking a flare with me, just in case. I also have a portable videophone with me, anyway."

Arl arched his dark and well-kept eyebrows in surprise.

"Looks like you're going to war, with all that gear."

Julia smiled; she had taken with her only the basic equipment of the Advanced Corps and realized she didn't feel the weight, even if the Sub-Commander appeared impressed by her stamina.

"I like to travel safely."

The man understood he wasn't going to receive a longer answer and pointed in front of him.

"The road is going to take a slight turn West, in the next 100 meters - there were some rocks on the North interfering with the trail."

"Very well, I'll remember it. See you soon."

Julia Dream

Captain Mayne turned westward and disappeared in the bushes.

∽

When the shadows closed behind her back, it finally dawned on her she had never found herself alone in the Forest. She cautiously observed the thick fern brushes, the huge wide tree trunks, the strong vines falling from the tallest branches. She was alert and concentrated, but not scared.

The light of the sun was filtered by the leaves, lighting up the dampness in the air like slanted columns of milky mist. Julia just stood there for minutes, perfectly still in the knot of vegetation, locking the stifling heat in a small portion of her mind, along with the trickle of sweat running down her spine.

She tried to absorb through observation news about the nature of the place, and slowly details started to take shape. She noticed the exposed roots, where a huge snake was crawling, dark tongue darting to and fro; the parrot that was keeping an eye on her from above, hidden in the leaves; the buzz of the insects in the bushes and the high cry of the squad of birds that flew past her.

She took a step forward with renewed awareness, and watched the snake slither behind the root and the parrot hop off to another branch. Her boot left no trace in the thick vegetation. She decided to move silently, and against the wind.

She walked for more or less half an hour, listening to the calls of the birds moving quickly from the tallest branches of the trees, old and gnarled - soon Julia noticed that the vegetation on her left looked even more luxuriant, and guessed there was probably a river nearby. A few steps away from two huge tree trunks she could see a clearing, a good arrival spot for a first exploration of the area.

She tilted her body to the left to peek in between the trees, when the birds suddenly interrupted their chatter.

From the entrance of the clearing, Julia freezes - she can see. The rustling of the branches, the fluttering wings of parrots flying away. She shoots.

A thud from above - a couple of heartbeats, and two inhuman screams pierce the afternoon as a thin and

deadly spear whistles in the air, digs deep in the fallen tree trunk, vibrating with reflected rage.

The Imperial rolls forward without even touching the ground with her back, dodges a second spear which flies above her head, stands up and shoots again; confused shots, and the Terrorist to the left falls down. The last one jumps at her from the right - Julia reacts but too late, falls on her back, all the weight and the yellow eyes of the creature on top of her. Her free external knee bends, extends in a kick - in the fraction of a second created by the new distance, a point blank shot, then silence.

Julia crawls out from under the Terrorist's corpse, and starts running.

∽

Arl was waiting for her with the electrocart, as agreed. She hurriedly jumped up, saying only one word, eyes fixed on the road.

"Fly."

The vehicle sprang forwards, rapidly gaining speed and darting between the trees. Julia caught her breath and composure while their distance with the border increased. Arl was looking at her from the corner of his eye, almost sardonically, but his smile faded as he noticed her attire and the girl's eyes becoming more and more lucid and cold. They didn't exchange a word until their arrival at the base.

"I have to speak with the Commander."

Julia's voice was molten steel.

"Now."

And she said it with such an intensity that the Sub-Commander, now frightened, darted off to find Nah.

It was soon clear that something had changed in the balance of power. Nah and Arl listened to Captain Mayne's report with wide eyes and tight lips.

"You're telling me you were forced to engage with the Terrorists in our territory? In broad daylight?"

Nah's voice, so confident and secure only a few hours earlier, was now shaken and hoarse with anxiety.

"Exactly. The border isn't holding. I believe those were scouts sent to consider the opportunity of following the river."

Sub-Commander Arl turned visibly white, and Nah turned her gaze on him.

"I think we would know if our vanguard had been seriously attacked - the Terrorists must have walked around it. Our network of outposts is clearly too spread out."

The sharp eyes of the Commander returned to Julia, lit by a new respect.

"You have my thanks for this crucial information, Captain. And my compliments for your awareness. Please accept my apologies, I had indicated that area as safe. I will send out Sum-Commander Arl to search the perimeter with a patrol squad."

"I can go with them to show them the way."

Nah shook her head, clearly wounded in her pride by what had happened.

"That won't be necessary. You have given us precise coordinates, and I don't want to distract you from your mission any longer. I will keep you updated on our discoveries."

Julia Dream

Julia addressed them with a tight bow, and left. She still had blood on her breastplate and dust in her hair.

◈

The unlikely and sudden sound of the videophone alert buzzed in the half-light of the room, arriving to the adjacent bathroom. Julia forced herself out of the shower, sketchily draping a towel around her figure and walking into the room to pick up the call.

"Julia?"

Marcus' voice and face, in direct access.

The girl appeared on screen, looking tired, with her hair wet. The Secretary smiled when she appeared.

"Hello there. Are you ok?"

"Not exactly. I almost got myself killed."

Marcus' smile faded in a second.

"What happened?"

"Terrorist scouts, in broad daylight, in full base territory. There were three of them and I was alone. I wanted to familiarize with the Forest when I bumped into their patrol."

Julia paused for a moment.

"I think the Terrorists are planning to enter the territory following the river. Commander Nah has been warned and has sent a squad there, where I had to engage and at the border, to make sure the barriers are holding."

Marcus nodded slowly, surprised but apparently not too upset by these news.

"Offer your help - you will be able to gather material even while fighting with them."

"That's what I thought, but I paused in front of her hurt pride. By the way, for the moment she has no proof of what happened if not my word."

"It's not up to you to worry about her feelings, just like she should not doubt your word."

Julia lowered her head.

"If I have done something wrong, I beg for your forgiveness."

"Don't worry. In any case once you meet again she'll know the truth of your story, and I believe she will appreciate the skills you can offer."

The Secretary looked at her in the eye.

"I think she will feel very lucky that you are there. She's probably considering that you can help her cut her losses by 50%."

Julia frowned, worried, but a new light glinted in her eyes.

"Can I really?"

"Of course you can. Choose a good team and collaborate with Nah."

The girl tightened her lips and nodded.

"I will."

∽

Once the videophone returned to nothing but a silver screen and Marcus' voice no longer filled the room, Captain Mayne quickly donned her armor, while angrily rubbing a towel against her now simply damp hair. She was sitting at the edge of the bed to pull on her boots, when she stopped for a moment, thoughtful, her hands on her knees and her gaze between her feet.

She stood up at last, stretching her knees first, then her torso, relaxing her back to place the palms of her hands on the floor, bent in two with her legs straight. She breathed out slowly, standing up only once she had completely emptied her lungs, then massaging the back of her neck and stretching her arms, elbows behind her head and the open palm of her hand on the opposite shoulder blade. She was ready.

A soldier, a grim looking girl, was waiting for her outside the door.

"Captain, the Commander has asked to see you."

Julia nodded, unsurprised.

"Very well, let's go."

The girl escorted her to Nah's tent, and at the entrance instead of taking the stairs up, they went through a metallic door dividing the rest of the ground floor from the entrance, and found themselves in a rectangular room. Nah was sitting at a table with other officers. Arl was not present.

"Commander, Captain Mayne has arrived."

With these words the girl saluted and left. Julia addressed a sign of salute to the room.

Nah pointed to a chair on her right.

"Captain, I hope you won't mind taking part in our meeting. We are grateful for the precious information on our enemy's movements you were able to provide."

Julia sat down, crossed her legs.

"Of course. You have all my support, if needed."

Julia Dream

The Commander's beautiful face relaxed, suggesting an emotion very similar to relief.

"Good. Here we have the directors of the Departments of Engineering, Fighters and Landmines, in order to organize a coordinated counterattack. From the border Arl has communicated that our outposts were never attacked – just a few skirmishes, probably diversions."

"Tell me about the Landmines Department."

A thin, dark haired man with lively eyes seated in front of Julia introduced himself.

"I'm Diego Leon, director of the Landmines Department. Our role is to draw a detailed map of this quadrant."

Nah nodded, stretching her legs forward and propping herself more comfortably on the chair.

"Some years before the Cataclysm, this area was filled with landmines by its inhabitants. Perhaps Secretary Marcus knows why. Anyway, even now that the radiation is gone, many still pose a threat of explosion."

"You want to push the Terrorists in the mined area?"

Leon's deep baritone answered her question.

"We had considered it, but it's not possible. Our knowledge of the area with landmines is still too scarce, and their disposition too irregular."

"I understand. Sorry if you have to repeat yourselves for me. What is your plan of action?"

"We have to counterattack. Penetrate deep in their territories and very carefully defend our borders."

Julia turned to look at the bulky man in his fifties that had spoken without introducing himself. She rapidly studied his confident posture, bordering overconfidence, taking in the sideways looks and raised eyebrows of his colleagues. Nah rapidly intervened.

"Yes, this is the idea. Director Vann's units are extremely well prepared, but we still have to understand how to deploy them most efficiently."

"I know several groups of Terrorists are converging in this area."

The Commander nodded, distractedly passing a hand through her hair.

"Yes, they are. The Forest is very thick and aerovehicle patrols reveal little of the Terrorists' movements. I'll have to send ahead an expert and quick group capable of penetrating deeply into their territory, while two larger groups will have to follow closely and constantly protect the rearguard to avoid an encirclement."

Julia nodded, her lips tight, eyebrows drawn in a concentrated expression.

"If the first group can remain unpredictable in its movements, it would probably have a constant initiative. I could merge my research group to this squad, if you wish."

Nah's green eyes met Julia's gray gaze, and the Commander nodded.

"Choose your men from any department between today and tomorrow. We'll have to leave in two days."

∽

"Captain Mayne."

Julia turned around, while crossing the entrance to the Commander's tent. Behind her, Diego Leon of the Landmines Department was hurrying to meet her.

"Captain, I'm going to the Operations Center of my Department to address our research to the areas which will soon interest us. Would you like to come with me? I will be able to explain our work better from there."

The man addressed a building on their right with a welcoming gesture of his hand.

Julia Dream

"My technicians are clearly at your disposal, should you want any in your team."

Julia looked up at the sun, enormous and glaring, dragging itself in its slow descent. Her head felt light because of the heat, of fatigue and the after-effect of adrenaline, but she forced herself to pay attention to the words of the officer facing her. Few hours remained before the sunset - it would appear unseemly to rest in such a time.

"Gladly. I take it your activity is fundamental."

The girl had spoken with sincere interest, and Leon's eyes flashed with satisfaction. Julia wondered whether the Landmines Department's work received the acknowledgement it deserved.

The man walked past her, walking in the shadow of the tent.

"Please, follow me. We'll be able to have something to drink once we are there."

Julia hurried after him. The Operational Center was no more than a hundred steps away from Commander Nah's tent, but the scorching air of the afternoon cut her breath. They hurried towards the cool and half-lit entrance of the warehouse with clear relief.

Julia Dream

Just at the door there was a refrigerator, with a small closet with some glasses; Leon took a pitcher full of pink liquid from the fridge and poured some for both.

"It's grapefruit juice. Very refreshing."

Julia took the glass to her lips, trying to grasp a smell, then took a small sip, surprised by the color of the liquid. The taste was sweet, sugary of concentrated sun, but with a sour aftertaste that rapidly quenched her thirst. Rapidly overcoming her hesitation she emptied the glass in a couple of gulps.

Leon had also finished his juice and was looking at her approvingly.

"The heat is intense in these hours. I wrote a procedure for my department, ordering to always have fluids at hand. With the humidity we have, it's easy to extract much of the water we need directly from the air."

Julia nodded, exploring the warehouse with her eyes. Several figures were sitting around about 20 interactive tables. A faint blue, green or brown luminescence came from the work stations.

"Fascinating. You seem extremely efficient. How do you work, exactly?"

Leon shrugged.

"Actually, a great part of our work is theory. We seek experimental confirmation when we can." Julia continued to look at him with interest, and after a moment the Director went on with his explanation.

"We start from air photography and try to understand where buildings stood, before the Cataclysm. At that point we simulate which adjacent areas could have been mined - when we can, we send probes in the suspicious area to confirm our interpretation."

The girl raised her eyebrows, impressed.

"That's an enormous task."

He smiled.

"Daunting, but not impossible. Several mines exploded during the Cataclysm, leaving traces that can simplify our task, when seen from up close."

"I understand."

"For our future mission, I plan to concentrate our search on the riverside. Please feel free to look around."

Julia nodded thoughtfully.

"Thank you, I will."

❧

Julia Dream

She silently walked around the perimeter of the warehouse. From the windows on the long sides of the rectangle she found weapon racks with guns and light rifles. It was quite obvious that units of the Landmine Department were on the field so rarely that there was no point in assigning them a personal weapon.

Julia picked up one of the rifles and some ammo from the shelf below. She loaded it, handled it with a few nervous gestures, then disassembled it and placed it back where it was - it almost looked like a toy when compared to her Kalashnikov Beta, but it was quick, easy to load and probably without recoil.

Looking up from the rack she realized she was being watched. A girl which looked Cleo's age or younger had left her workstation to come closer, and was looking at her.

Julia opened her eyes to study the unlikely subject in front of her. The figure stood against the light, but her profile was unique: her light hair was tied in two pigtails at the side of her head – by two pink bands, as appeared when she moved closer, crossing the space lit by the window in front of Julia. Her nails were long, enameled, pearly and perfect, while her feet were tucked in a pair of clogs open on the toes.

Quite obviously the Landmines Department didn't care much about uniform.

The girl spoke with a voice ringing with curiosity and shyness combined.

"Hello! How are you? The Landmines Department is amazing, don't you think? It's always like working on a treasure hunt."

The sound of a weight falling with a thud on the carpet of ferns. The smell of the shot, red stains on a body that is projected away, blood stains on the grass, on the flowers. The blaming silence of the entire Forest, of the tall silent trees.

"I had to shoot three Terrorists today. And I'm planning operations that probably will lead me to shoot at many others. How do you think I feel?"

The blonde girl changed color at these words, going pale before blushing, even though Julia's tone had been tired rather than hostile. Understanding the effect of her words the Captain sweetened her tone.

Julia Dream

"What is your name?"

"Ary Lee, Ma'am."

"Can I call you Ary?"

"As you wish, Ma'am."

"What has led you to join the Army, Ary?"

"My brother, or better, my brother's example. He is 5 years older than me and has been at the front since I was a kid. I never wanted to be a shame for my family, so I followed his footsteps as soon as I could."

Julia looked at her in silence, curious, waiting for her to keep on talking.

"From the Ministry's tests I discovered my inclination towards the Landmines Department's work, so here I am in B007."

"Do you know the riverside area well?"

Ary's pigtails jumped up and down when she nodded vigorously.

"Oh yes. I carried out the studies of Geographical History on the riverbed, to understand where it used to run at the time of the Cataclysm."

Julia narrowed her eyes, careful, speaking slowly.

"In two days I'm going to be leaving for a mission in that area. I'm going to take with me specialists from the different departments. Do you want to come with me?"

The eyes of the young researcher shone.

"Yes! If the Director has nothing against it."

"I'll speak with him, I don't think there will be any issue. Find me someone that can act as your backup."

Ary's pigtails seemed almost to droop down at the sudden terror that flashed in her eyes, as if the risks had finally dawned on her in hearing talks about a backup.

Captain Mayne stared at her unflinching, in silence - after a few seconds the blonde girl bowed her head, whispering and trying to hide her shame.

"I'm not very good at shooting."

Finally Julia smiled at her.

"That is not a problem. The Fighters' team will take care of that."

᪥

Sprawled on the bed with arms and legs pointing at the four corners of the room, Julia was debating with her insomnia. Her muscles, heavy with fatigue and adrenaline, demanded an unconditional and undisturbed sleep - but her mind was working, following the tasks ahead of her. Find a full team; she was still missing two engineers and at least five fighters. Agree with the Commander on how many units to employ as a vanguard, along with the team of technicians. Carry out Marcus' mission and concurrently safeguard Nah's needs. And then talk to Cleo. This was what made Captain Mayne toss and turn in her bed. Her body demanded rest, but her mind needed a vent. At last, in the safety of the base and in the darkness of the night hours, the unexpected risk of the encounter with the three Terrorists appeared as it had been - enormous. And now that Julia had carried out with due diligence the ordinary and extraordinary tasks of the day, she felt the need to share without shame all her posthumous fear.

For Nah or Arl or for anyone in the base her death would mean nothing more than a bunch of annoying papers to fill, but pouring her fear on Cleo was not a viable option. She curled up and hugged her knees, anticipating the version of the story she would tell her sister; slowly she let her consciousness slip.

❦

Julia Dream

When she opened her eyes, the sun was already filtering in the room through the steel shielding at the window. Dusty and fierce rays were drawing shining stains of molten gold in the silent half-light of the room.

Julia sighed. She turned on her right side and closed her eyes, mentally counting the ten seconds she had conceded herself before getting up. She relaxed all her muscles before sitting up and raising mechanically. She looked at her image in the bathroom mirror, straightened her shoulders, splashed water in her semi-closed eyes - another day was starting for Captain Mayne.

∽

Vann, Director of the Fighters, was observing the morning drill of his men, shielding his eyes with one of his hands. The sun, enormous and menacing, made the fighter's faces and arms shiny with sweat while they engaged in combat exercises.

Next to the man's massive figure Julia appeared incredibly small and lithe, yet her pose was attentive and martial - the way she held her hands behind her back, and her tight and concentrated eyes contrasted with the relaxed demeanor of the Director. The girl's attention darted from one work group to the other, trying to grasp the entire scene, while clearly Vann only had eyes for his favorite pupil.

After all, he was hard to miss – tall and muscular, he was in the front row, with his straight nose and the well-defined jaw of someone used to being satisfied. He was resisting without effort to his sparring partner's attacks, and Vann was looking him with a half smile of scarcely hidden smugness. For a moment Julia wondered about the familiarity in his looks, before realizing it was his attitude which reminded her of Kob.

"Eorg, come here!"

The fighter broke out from his group at his director's call, and while he was approaching Vann finally spoke to Julia, still smiling.

"Eorg is the best of his class. He's coming in this mission with you."

Julia tightened her lips, and said nothing.

Eyes meet. A pair does not see the Captain but a woman, is not interested in the words or gestures of

the Director but in the features of a face, the details of a uniform - the rays connecting the throat collar to the armor neckline, the line of the trousers on the hips.

Pupils dilating at the sudden and long buried memory of another life, of a school mate and a natural and unthinking attraction, effusions in the school restrooms.

Eyes that become a darker gray as the memory fades.

❧

The team had been summoned in the conference clearing in front of the North door, and was now fidgeting nervously, half-blinded by the low and light clouds which were multiplying the natural reflection of the sun.

Unseen, Julia was watching from a pavilion on the side. She was studying the controlled fear of Ary Lee, who anxiously looked at the weapon on her side from time to time, probably trying to get used to it. She took note of the blatant and solid arrogance of Eorg and of the meticulous appearance – and tired faces - of the engineers chosen for this mission by the director of their department.

After a couple of minutes she walked out of the shadow to appear suddenly behind the surprised team, walking up to face them and look at all of them in the eye. She spoke in a low voice, her eyes concentrated, index and middle finger of her left hand pulling at a pellicle of her thumb in a subconscious sign of nervousness.

"Two things."

Ten anxious pairs of eyes stared at her in a dense silence.

"We are going to be the front line. If anyone wants to pull back, now is the time."

Worried looks and dragging of boots, but no answer.

"Good. Second point. For your own good, I expect you to do exactly as I tell you."

Ary Lee nodding in the background, flashes in the eyes of the engineers and Eorg. Julia graced them with a tense smile.

"In the full respect of your specific competence, clearly."

She flopped down on the floor with her legs crossed, signaling with her hand for the team to follow her example. The new faces were the engineers, two men in their forties that had clearly spent the night studying with the Department the river and its currents in order to provide assistance in building bridges and rafts; and Ary Lee's backup, who introduced himself as First Analyst Ow. He was a tall man with a stern gaze, clearly experienced, and Julia welcomed him warmly, sending an encouraging smile to a withdrawn and thoughtful Ary.

Along the fighters chosen by Julia, the imposing figure of soldier 'Rrla stood out; she was a strong black woman, almost as tall as Eorg and just as muscular, making Captain Mayne appear extremely light and thin in comparison. She wasn't saying a word, but appeared to avoid looking in Eorg's direction.

Julia nodded silently, trying to grasp as quickly as possible the first signs of the group's dynamics. Her group.

∼⑥

She was walking the corridor to her module, with the flowing of time in her ears and the certainty she was being followed at a close distance in the long metal desert. She recognized without turning her head Eorg's heavy footsteps and slowed down slightly, while the furrow of a frown formed on her forehead.

And then the unexpected and compact mass of 50 kg of muscle throws Eorg against the gray and opaque wall, with one of Captain Mayne's thighs jammed between his legs to pin him down.

The left hand grabs his hair at the nape of his neck, the other one pulls him by the collar in a deep and fierce kiss that does not give or take, but consumes.

Finally Julia detaches her lips and doubles her grip, pushing elbow and forearm against his chest, nailing her shining eyes on Eorg's bewildered face.

"Is this what you want?"

She lets go of the grip with a small push after 30, 40 seconds of silence.

She smiles/nods.

"Look somewhere else."

Captain Mayne watched the Fighter's retreat for a few seconds, then Eorg became a distant thought dismissed in some dark basement of her mind.

She stared at the videophone for a long time, searching for the right words to explain her imminent departure to Cleo.

Finally, she found enough courage to dial the number. Despite the parade of optimism she received, it was the echo of Cleo's worried voice that filtered in the Captain's dreams.

VIII

Layers of dust on weapons and equipment told the tale of the time elapsed since the day of their departure. Julia squinted, remembering the effort it had required to remain impassible, despite the fatigue, the nagging aftertaste of the now unusual synthetic food, Nah's inquisitive eyes and the goose bumps on her arms seeing the imperial flags waving for the occasion.

She mechanically brushed back a strand of hair away from her sweaty forehead. Even the bodice of the armor was opaque with brownish dust, like her entire figure and the team's tired faces. They were walking in single file, with the Captain in front and Eorg in the rearguard; they had separated from Arl's contingent to deeply penetrate in enemy territory with the light of the day. Julia had decided to leave behind the electrocarts with the Engineers and 'Rrla, venturing in to explore on foot with the hope of having a chance to record some sounds in case of an encounter. Her group knew that the main objective of their mission was to gather information for the

Department of Knowledge of the Ministry of Counter-Terrorism.

She halted the small line behind her, raising a gloved hand - the tallest treetops were moving, but it was only the wind. She closed her eyes to concentrate on the sounds. The rustle of the leaves. The creaking of branches. The far cry of a distant bird.

The Captain let her arm fall down, turning back. She found the wary and quizzical eyes of the group staring at her. The shoulders of the fighters were tense, the posture rigid, faces sweaty but pale: the Forest and the heat were taking their toll.

And yet, the Captain herself appeared to be gaining energy day by day. In less than a week Julia had already regained color, muscle and tone. When her head started to spin, she didn't show it.

She looked back once at the thick vegetation.

"We're heading back."

Ⳝ

Julia and Arl were sitting on camp chairs placed around a small and wobbly table, straining to keep them straight on the harsh terrain. Around them the team was preparing the camp for the night.

The Captain was shaking her head, her short but thick black hair waving around.

"There's no point in going during the day. The Terrorists have spotted us and are already on guard. I will have to go scouting during the night. Tomorrow."

The Sub-Commander tightened his lips, worried.

"We want them to move out. If they do so without a direct contact the better."

Julia nodded.

"You are correct. But I have different orders. I will go with my team."

Arl hesitated for a moment, undecided, then appeared reassured by her smile.

"Don't worry, I won't need back up."

The Captain elegantly rose from her chair, walking towards the electrocart guarded by Ary Lee. The girl's blonde pigtails were a slightly droopy and tangled, her eyes staring at nothing, or perhaps following the distant bickering between 'Rrla and Eorg.

Julia sat by her side.

"Are you ok?"

Ary Lee jumped up, startled. She opened her mouth as if wanting to say something, then closed it shut, even though her damp eyes spoke for her. A new note appeared in Julia's voice, the note of someone asking a question that demands an answer.

"Ary Lee, what is going on? Consider this conversation informal for now."

The blonde wiped her tears, hiding her eyes in the palms of her hands for a moment. She spoke in a controlled voice. "I feel terribly inadequate. And I am scared."

Julia stared at her for a few seconds, with no expression whatsoever. Then she sighed and shook her head – and while Ary Lee was by now expecting a harsh rebuke, Captain Mayne sent her a crooked smile.

"You are appropriate for the task because I chose you, and you accepted. And it is healthy to feel fear."

Julia rose, observing the orange ball of the sun setting through the branches of the Forest. She tapped on Ary's shoulder.

"Be prepared, tomorrow night we'll go scouting and I want you to come with me."

"I know all of you are going to be there to protect me."

Julia's smile broadened.

172

"Good."

Ary Lee was looking at her with an unexpressed question in her eyes. She finally found the heart to pose it, lowering her eyes.

"Captain? We are all scared. More or less, in a more blatant or hidden manner. Except for you."

Julia tensed, struck by a deep malaise, slapped in the face by the evidence of the fact that what she feared the most was the violence of the Empire, rather than the natural fierceness of an enemy defending its territory. It dawned on her that she breathed more freely in the midst of the dangers of the wild Forest than in the familiar and crushing structure of society.

She just allowed herself a couple of seconds before answering. She deleted the first answer that had come to her mind.

"This is my problem."

The second answer, far from being trivial, concealed a deeper truth.

"I have been trained to not feel it."

∽

The Captain had insisted on having Ary Lee at her side during the first night recon, for reasons which went far beyond simple psychological considerations. Some areas that had once been mined were easy to recognize – depressions in the ground characterized by younger trees – but other spots were more treacherous.

Ary Lee knew how to estimate the distance between trees and determine whether an unusual open space was too big due to the metal ions of a mine tampering with the growth of a seed. The girl calculated with concentration and with a precision that was constantly backed up by First Analyst Ow; focus on the job kept her fear at bay.

Hours had passed since their departure at sunset and the moonlight was starting to filter through the treetops, when Julia suddenly turned around to stare in the darkness to her left. The leaves of branch were slightly vibrating.

"Turn all the lights on! Fan them out!"

The second the lights turned on, the silence was broken by cries and repetitive thuds against the tree trunks. A small vibration confirmed the recording device Julia was carrying attached to her belt had activated itself.

174

Julia Dream

The girl turned around immediately, whispering quickly.

"Stay here. Eorg, 'Rrla, cover me.'"

She sprinted in the woods following the sounds, checking the treetops and darting around the trunks, the Forest incredibly still in the powerful light of the beacons. 2, 3, 5, 10 seconds of silence, then a new rhythm answering the first call.

A muscle on Eorg's biceps twitched as he strengthened his grip on the gun; 'Rrla's dark eyes nervously darted from left to right. Julia froze, listening to the beat of her heart more than she was actually paying attention to the Terrorist's message – half a minute at the most, before a renewed and spectral silence.

The recorder stopped its vibration, and the Captain started breathing again.

"Go, go, go!"

❧

"How did you know we had been spotted?"

Eorg's voice resonated in Arl's camp, friendly but high and curious. The fighter immediately won himself reproachful looks and an aura of silence surrounded him after this clear violation of protocol. Julia decided to ignore this since he was insisting, clearly interested.

"Really, there was nothing there when you turned to look."

The Captain smiled.

"Exactly, there was no wind either. But the leaves were rustling."

"Oh."

Eorg appeared satisfied with the answer and nodded. Julia quickly checked the electrocart that was being loaded with the material they would need for their daylight scouting, and gestured for her team to gather. She sat on the floor, followed by the rest of the team.

"Two things."

While speaking, she made sure her eyes embraced the entire semicircle that had formed around her.

"Good job tonight, everyone. Our timing was perfect."

A pause, the time needed to take in the smiles of the group.

"Now, the guidelines for tomorrow. Our mission is to gather information, I don't want to fight if not to defend ourselves. We are exploring, not going to battle."

The team nodded, and almost as if all of them had exhaled the tension and the stress of an unusual situation, Captain Mayne suddenly noticed the stale scent of sweat and fear.

She stood up, thus closing the brief meeting.

"One last thing. Tomorrow before we leave I want all of you to go through the disinfection procedure. I don't want our smell giving us away."

❦

The place was the same, but Ary's cartography was needed to confirm it. The compact light of the day, the bright colors and the constant chattering of birds made it completely unrecognizable since their encounter with the Terrorist sentinel.

"It is highly likely there is a Terrorist encampment nearby. I want to find it."

Impassable faces, eyes full of concern. Captain Mayne ignored them to stare once again through the leaves.

"Follow me, and keep silent – Ary Lee, right behind me. I need to know if the way is safe."

They found the Terrorist camp not far away, taking a turn towards the river. They cautiously peered in a small clearing which according to Ary's calculations had probably formed after the detonation of ancient landmines - some of the branches of the tallest trees, twisted or cut, formed rough huts.

The village looked like it had been abandoned in a hurry, but Julia, perfectly still in her armor, observed the borders of the clearing. She kept her team waiting, barely mouthing her instructions.

"Don't move. Look for signs of a trap or an ambush."

Ary Lee and her colleague Ow immediately entered a state of relaxed concentration, their minds trained to grasp all environmental detail – only the fighters showed the anxiety this forced pause caused them, and even the usually impassible 'Rrla kept combing her hands through her long, wavy hair, or wiping her forehead with her sleeve.

Finally the Captain's voice broke the silence.

"Ow, report in."

"Seven intact huts. Traces of at least two that have been dismantled or destroyed. Their structural appearance suggests they are layered with leather in the inside and leaves on the outside, with some walls directly connected to the tree trunks. There is a circle of stones in the middle, probably for campfires."

Ow raised his eyes to the trees before continuing.

Julia Dream

"There are no indicators of hidden presence or traps in the vegetation. The shadows we see on the ground are consistent with what we see at first sight."

Julia nodded.

"Very well. We're going in. I don't want anyone to fire if not for immediate defense."

She searched for 'Rrla's eyes.

"Stay here with Ow and Ary. The rest with me."

Boot prints in the red earth of the clearing. Julia moves sideways, in silence, clockwise.

A shuffling rustle from a tent – the violent flare of a gun, the genuine scream of a woman.

"NO!"

Julia pushes away Eorg's weapon, deviating and stopping the trajectory, runs towards the lacerated hut, the external leaves now lying on the floor, the internal leathers shattered and torn.

Captain Mayne yanks at an extremity with anger, exposes the figure of one of the Terrorist women, sprawled backwards and bleeding, eyes closed in her beautiful and apparently completely human face.

"They must have left her behind because she was sick. Look at how swollen her belly is."

Julia is now bent over the woman, placing two delicate fingers on her throat. No pulse. She imposes silence with a sign of her hands, speaks without even looking at Eorg in the face.

"She was pregnant."

White in the face, Julia closes her eyes, swallows saliva and tears. Opens and closes her fists before turning around to look at the soldier – sweat beading on his forehead. Words that are little more than a hiss.

"You have no idea of what you have just done."

Captain Mayne breathes out, lets the tent fall back.

"We're going back."

Quick paces up to the edge of the clearing.

୶

The Captain had shut herself in one of the tents of Arl's camp, in utter silence. The sun was starting to set in the green horizon of the Forest when Ary Lee finally reached the accommodation, shuffling her feet in embarrassment.

"Captain Mayne?"

"Come in, Ary Lee."

Julia's voice had lost the steely note of her rage and sounded simply tired, even through the muffling effect of the tent.

The Advanced Corps Captain was sitting on a chair and staring into the void, her legs crossed, silently waiting for the intruder to explain her presence. She hadn't even taken off her armor.

The blonde of the Mines Department stared at the ground.

"Are you going to court martial Eorg?"

Julia allowed the girl to hear her sigh.

"Why, is he plotting his escape?"

Ary Lee looked up, suddenly terrified.

"No, absolutely not! I didn't mean..."

"That was ironic. I don't see many places where he could be running, anyway."

She softened her tone, seeing the appalled expression on the white and tired face of the girl.

"I'm not going to, in any case. I will not hand him to a special tribunal, even though he would deserve it. But I have to send him away from the team."

IX

Marcus' face was concentrated, his fingers playing with a pen he was jostling between his long fingers.

"During the last two weeks I have gathered several samples, as required. The last ten days have been particularly fruitful."

Julia's tone was set on ministerial professionalism, but the days spent in the front lines in the Forest had left their mark. She had two scratches on her cheek, a completely bruised elbow and the rigid posture of sore shoulders.

"I have recordings of Terrorists fleeing, Terrorists raising some kind of alarm, or deciding to engage. I picked up the samples in different territories, in order to test what should be different groups."

Marcus nodded, smiling at her.

"Good. I had no doubt."

Julia shifted her shoulders.

"I ask for permission to return to the Base. Two of my fighters are wounded, even though not dangerously. And I had to send soldier Eorg back to his department."

The Secretary leaned forward on the chair, dropping the pen and crossing his arms on the desk.

"Is he one of the wounded?"

"No."

Julia sighed and once again Marcus encouraged her.

"The unofficial report will do for the moment."

On the other side of the videophone the girl closed her eyes for a brief moment, but opened them soon after, an intense gray gaze.

"He fired without waiting for my order, with very grave consequences. He killed one of the Terrorist women, unarmed, not aggressive and very pregnant."

Marcus's eyes opened with surprise, then he sadly shook his head.

"What an idiot! We have lost a great occasion... if only we could have had the chance of raising one of their children..."

Julia nodded, crestfallen.

"I know."

"What was such an element doing in your team, anyway?"

There was no accusation in the tone, yet Captain Mayne tensed all the same and bowed her head.

"I would never have chosen him. But he is, or perhaps was, the pupil of his director's eye, who basically pushed him on me. To refuse him could have created a diplomatic incident with Nah."

Julia pressed her lips in an expression of contained frustration.

"That day he was at my side exactly because I wanted to keep him under control."

The Secretary let out a sigh.

"You did all you could. And the official report?"

"Soldier Eorg has manifested muscular tremors, concentrated at the height of the wrist and the hand, which caused accidental fire. He therefore should undergo immediate medical analysis. Before that, he is absolutely not fit to carry a gun."

Marcus raised his eyebrows with a half smile.

"Diplomatic and wise choice."

"I was taught how to lie with style at the Ministry."

Julia almost rushed her hand to her lips, immediately regretting the thought that had slipped out, with the help of her fatigue – but Marcus burst out laughing.

"Right."

Julia Dream

The Secretary observed her again, his eyes shining with something similar to affection.

"Return to the base Julia, and rest. We will reconvene soon."

꧁

Captain Mayne's team crossed the gates of OB07 two days later. Faces were calm, but the group was silent. They were leaving behind them a front that was still open, with constant skirmishes. Besides Eorg, officially dismissed for medical visits, Julia's team had not suffered losses, but it was well known in the base that some scouts from the main contingent had never returned.

A small curious crowd had formed near the electrocart hangar. Commander Nah was striding towards them, sweeping her blond hair behind her ears with a brush of her hand.

Julia jumped down from the electrocart even before it stopped, impatiently but gracefully. She looked at her team with bright eyes.

"You are free to return to your departments. Our mission is over."

She allowed herself a smile, before turning her back to them and attend to her formal duties with the Commander.

"Excellent job, all of you."

She had no time to listen to their replies, which were left hanging unsaid in the air, like dust in a ray of light. Nah had reached her side.

"Captain."

Julia read a silent question and a sense of urgency in the intelligent eyes of the woman standing in front of her.

"Please, follow me. Secretary Marcus was waiting for your arrival."

౼

Julia found it hard not to smile when knocking at the door of the module assigned to Marcus. The corners of her mouth fell when she suddenly felt like a pang the absence of Cleo, in the familiarity of the context, but the warmth in Marcus's voice restored her good mood.

"Come in."

She opened the door with a renewed smile on her face.

"Secretary."

She addressed him with a formal bow, but he answered her smile, gesturing her to take a seat and cutting formalities short.

"Julia! It's good to see you smiling."

"I admit I am happy to see you, Secretary."

"Have you forgiven me?"

She suddenly returned serious and pressed her lips together, thinking.

"Yes, I suppose I have."

A pause, then she started talking in a lighter tone.

"I didn't expect to find you here."

Marcus relaxed, falling back against the chair. The entrance to his module was furnished as a study, with two chairs and a small table.

"I'm here for several reasons. First of all, I wanted to check on your health status."

Julia raised her eyebrows.

"I found you dangerously tired when we spoke and wanted to check your condition in person. I'm pleased to find you are already better."

He raised index and middle finger to form a 2.

"Secondly, I wanted Nah to see me and remember that the Empire has not forgotten this base and follows the situation carefully. This has given me a chance to form an opinion for myself."

Julia tilted her head, waiting for the conclusion.

"Finally, I'm here for your next mission."

Marcus allowed himself a small sigh.

"Finish what you started. Help the Commander and Sub-Commander Arl secure their territory. The recordings you have should suffice."

He studied the girl's blank face.

"Two weeks, that's all. Rest tomorrow and yet another day if you feel you need it."

Captain Mayne nodded in silence.

"Julia, I know you don't like to kill. That's another reason why you're the right person for this. I need this to be surgical and controlled, the Terrorists so near and unpredictable are a danger, as you have seen. You can save the lives of some of Nah's people."

She sighed, shaking her head slightly.

"No need to convince me, Secretary. You know I don't have much of a choice, and that I would obey anyway."

His dark eyes were almost sad when they set on Julia's face, already directed towards the door to leave.

"I know, but I believe convincing you adds value to the result. We'll have the opportunity to talk about freedom of choice some day, perhaps."

Julia turned around and smiled at him, now curious.

"Gladly."

And left, closing the door with a light rustle.

~§

Long ringing, and finally Cleo, ruffled hair and red eyes. A male leg moves out of the quadrant of the videophone.

"Hi Cleo! Did I interrupt something?"

"No, don't worry. Dreas and I were talking and it took me a while to answer. It's late at night here."

Captain Mayne frowns, kissed by the golden morning light.

"How is it possible? It's morning here..."

A quick overseas smile.

"It's because of the Earth's rotation, of which face is turned to the Sun – if you move parallel to the equator, the Sun will rise in a different moment."

"Oh. I am sorry I disturbed you."

"Don't worry. When are you coming back?"

Hope lights a spark in the eyes, brightens the tone of voice.

"In two weeks or so. Will you introduce me to Dreas then?"

Cleo nods absentmindedly, peers in her sister's tired eyes.

"Where are they sending you for these days?"

"To do a less dangerous and dirtier job."

A determined answer, a multicolored voice of warmth and sadness.

"I'll be waiting."

᪥

Ten days later the name of Captain Julia Mayne echoed in all the Departments of the base, anticipating her return. It rang in the orders written and countersigned with the special protocol she had sent from the front, emerged in whispers from mess hall and dorms, in conversations from strategic meetings.

Initially in the first village she had carried out a traditional, daylight strike – later she had decided to attack during the night, tearing away from the enemy's control even their best hours. She had set to deforest and immediately create paths in the conquered territories. Rumors had it she had pushed an entire village in a zone covered by a major alert from the Landmines Department. Pushing beyond the official line of conquest, many camps had already been abandoned. It was said that in this case the Captain would order to carefully take down all the Terrorist tents, gathering all abandoned effects in numbered bags. In the wake of her path, it was as if those villages had never existed.

X

The column of electrocarts was raising a conspicuous amount of dust.

The world is now eyes squinting in the sunlight, wind in her hair, red and thin earth in her nostrils. Julia is standing on the vehicle at the center of the column, crossing kilometers of enemy territory with blaring music in her ears, and hears no one.

"Captain."
Reading lips, she unplugged her earphones, holding in a sigh.
"Captain, the head vehicle is communicating that we are in sight of the base."
Julia pinched her mouth in something like a smile.
"Good."
The officer that had spoken looked at her curiously.
"Shall I stop the convoy, Captain? Don't you wish to take the leading vehicle?"

Julia Dream

Pause – then Captain Mayne did a gesture which looked a lot like a shrug, her face expressionless.

"I guess I should."

❧

So that was how Julia made her entrance in OB07, standing on a jump seat of the front vehicle and welcomed upon her arrival by a small crowd of colleagues and curious. She recognized Eorg and Ary Lee's smile nearby in the front row – and only then did she realize that the base had been afraid, and her attack on the Terrorists was experienced like a liberation.

She had no time for surprise, being met by Nah and Arl who were striding towards the electrocart hangar. Julia jumped down to greet them, slightly shaking because of the absence of the now familiar vibration of the vehicle. Nah ignored her fatigue.

"On time as usual, Captain. Excellent job. An airship is waiting for you."

Julia opened her mouth but had no time to speak.

"I have taken the liberty to board all your baggage and equipment. You will be able to change comfortably on board."

The Captain followed the two out of the hangar, forcing away a chill of a dark and hidden fear. She suddenly looked extremely tired.

Arl sent an apologetic smile in her direction.

"The airship has orders to depart as soon as possible."

❧

The wings of the gigantic aerovehicle shone like the feathers of a fire bird, the solar micropanels covering them already oriented and whirring. Forests, lakes, oceans swept past the vast double window. Secretary Marcus and Captain Mayne sat at a small table, sipping orange juice from elegant chalices. Julia looked like a kid, dressed in civilian garb and flopped down on the soft seat in an asymmetric pose, disorderly and not at all martial. Marcus was smiling.

"They decided to get you out of the base as soon as possible because your fame was growing too much. Nah must have considered that your skills on the field could undermine her authority, especially with the new contingent I brought in with the airship."

The Secretary's eyes lit up as he grinned.

"She would have kept me from coming out of the ship if she could. I opted to stay on board because I didn't want to unnerve her."

Julia eyes flashed, her lips clenched - Marcus was quick to grasp the unexpressed comparison.

"I know. We have demanded a lot from you. But now you will have a chance to rest."

"Do you know anything of my next assignment?"

The Secretary shook his head.

"I don't know anything about it. I know that your results have attracted the attention of my colleagues at the Ministry, but we all agree you need at least 10 days of rest."

Julia raised her eyebrows, but Marcus kept on with a stern voice.

"You need them, Julia. Even if you weren't seriously wounded, you have gone through prolonged stress. And you have a fever."

"What?"

"You are obviously feverish. Skintilla must have done an excellent job in ingraining combat as a second nature, if you didn't even notice. Nonetheless, you shouldn't ignore the signals your body sends you."

Captain Mayne remained silent, straightening up on the seat and checking her sore spots through that simple movement. She noted the alteration in her pulse, the lightheaded feeling, the concentration she needed for the simplest gestures – symptoms she had downplayed as simple fatigue.

She forced herself to relax as much as possible.

⁖

Two days of rest, which end with the shrill ringing of duty's call.

Marcus' face is tense, his voice blank.

"My regards, Captain. The Ministry has decided on your next assignment."

Hands behind her back in a courteous stance, Julia digs the nails of her fingers in her palms, acknowledging the formal tone. Monitored conversation.

"At your orders, Secretary."

"An inspection in OB26. More details will be provided during your journey to destination."

Julia shakes. A vibration which starts from the abdomen, embraces the hips, discharges through the arms. The Captain hides her wrath with a deep bow, and Marcus rapidly closes the communication.

ક

"What happened?"

"Nothing."

"Don't bullshit me."

Julia averted her eyes from her sister's concerned face.

"They are asking me to perform an inspection. In OB26."

Cleo narrowed her eyes, which flashed almost metallically, and for a moment all the resemblance and the blood bond with Captain Mayne shone through her sweet features as they were suddenly hardened by rage.

When she spoke her voice was dripping a deep and unimaginable hatred.

"Bastards."

Julia Dream

❦

Bastards. Offspring of wretches without honor and marred by shame. Julia agreed with the definition, and yet only extremely high ranking personalities of the Empire could override Marcus like that.

The Captain's stare crossed the window without even seeing the beautiful scenery of the dawn on the sea, the same scenery that had moved her to tears the first time she had gazed upon it. But now Julia's eyes were dry with insomnia. Thoughts fleeted on her forehead like parakeets flying in the American Forest.

Her mind was on the viciousness of the test they were proposing to her this time, and yet she felt a pang of affection for Marcus – it was clear he had nothing to do with this. She thought of Cleo and her strange relationship with Dreas, a tall fellow with darting eyes that had been obviously scared by Captain Mayne. And then she thought of OB26.

Only fire and flames behind her closed eyes, flashes never seen but very often imagined, in the belly of buried dreams and illicit divagations of the mind.

She placed her right hand on her stomach, as if it could somehow calm the heartburn. She had decided not to report the problem, knowing that the doctors were bound to convey to central control information on the health of the officers.

And she knew the origin of her sickness very well. Of all the Operational Bases of the Empire, they had sent her to inspect the one where her parents had died.

&

In high uniform, Captain Mayne paraded the moons of her rank and let her loose hair fall back at the sides of her face, almost to her shoulders. She had underlined the ice in her eyes with black make-up.

She descended from the aerovehicle's stairs keeping her back straight and grasping a pen and a notebook her hand, immediately noticing the absence of the Commander of the base and the nervous shuffling of the underling who represented him in a clumsy welcoming party.

The errand boy graced her with an attempt to start a conversation and a nervous smile.

Julia Dream

"It's an honor for us to welcome you in OB26, Captain. Did you know this base has been attested here for ten years?"

"9 years and 4 months, to be precise. I've read the papers."

The smile on the bureaucrat's face froze for a moment, while Julia grinned showing her white teeth and pointy canines.

"I have also read of the fire."

"Na-Naturally. May I show you to your rooms, to see if they are pleasing to you, Captain?"

"No. I want to see the Commander."

"The Commander is currently bu..."

"I will wait."

❧

Julia waited at the entrance door of Commander Rossis's rooms for 20 minutes, standing perfectly still, exactly at the center of the recording field of the camera placed above the doorpost. The device would transmit to the Commander her impassable demeanor and the rising anxiety of her escort.

Once the door opened it was immediately clear, through telltale semi-closed eyes and ruffled hair, that the

Commander had not found it necessary to wake up to greet the inspector. Someone very clearly had just dragged him out of bed.

Captain Mayne looked at the half-open collar and dirty boots of the man and her gray eyes flared in a face that was otherwise as blank as her tone.

"Good morning, Commander Rossis."

"To you, Captain..."

"Mayne."

No reaction to the name from Rossis, total indifference. Julia forced herself to silence.

"You have to forgive me if I have kept you waiting, I was indisposed yesterday evening and..."

Julia raised her eyebrows, with a great show of concern.

"Oh? Would you like me to come with you to the base infirmary?"

The wrinkles on the older man's face – he must have been in his sixties – doubled with his worried expression. The Captain could feel that her interlocutor had stopped breathing for a moment, caught by surprise.

"No, no. I am well now. No need."

"Excellent. I would still like to visit the medical section of the base. It seems like it was the most damaged by the fire three years ago, was it not?"

Rossis scoffed.

"I don't remember the details of the damage, I seem to remember something of the sort from the Technical Report of the Engineering Department, right after the event."

"Yes, I have read it and that is what it says. Perhaps the Engineering Department will be able to provide more details."

With a deliberate and calculated pause, Julia averted her eyes for a moment, only to bring them back up and pin the Commander to the wall with her stare.

"And yet I am surprised you would not remember. 3 years are not a very long time, and 19 dead in an accident... too many."

Rossis puffs up, goes red, raises an offended voice.
"I haven't lost any of my men!"
No reaction on the girl's face.
"Really? Interesting."
And the Commander starts sweating with fear.

Julia Dream

Captain Mayne smiled again.

"I believe I will examine my room now."

᠗

In the following days, the dark profile of the inspector became a silent and disquieting presence haunting OB26. Julia was quick, elusive and sharp as a sword.

Despite declaring her intentions to Rossis, three days passed before she knocked at the door of Director Rian, of the Engineering Department. He was curiously young for his position, but apparently much more professional than his Commander. Julia felt she owed him a warning.

"Director, before we start our conversation, I want you to know that it will be recorded for our files."

The man nodded gravely, and she went on.

"I have read you landed this position after the fire. I have also studied the current security procedures. Did you write them?"

The young director pursued his lips and narrowed his eyes.

"Yes and no."

"They are perfect. Had they been applied at the time of the fire, there would have been no casualties. And yet I find myself with 19 dead and a shadowy report. I want the truth."

A sigh.

"The current procedures, besides some small updates, had been elaborated by Director Evy with my contribution, before the fire. At the time Commander Rossis refused to ask for the equipment we needed to implement them. After the fire, out of fear that Evy could reveal what had happened, Rossis had her transferred and appointed me to be the Director – I was young, inexperienced and malleable. I would guess this was his wager. What matters is that Director Evy bartered her silence with the adoption of the current procedures and the equipment we needed to make them effective."

"Very interesting. Is there anything else I should know?"

The Director shook his head, smiled ruefully.

"Not that I know. I have already said enough for Rossis to ask for my head."

Captain Mayne smiled dryly.

"Don't worry about that. My files are private, and I believe that in the near future the Commander will have other occupations rather than thinking of transferring you. After all, you have only confirmed what I was already thinking."

∽

Under a violet sky heavy with clouds, sunset was an intense orange stripe on the horizon. Only one visit now remained, the last one, to give her the time to build up her courage. The medical section was located at a distance from the center of the base: about ten dorm modules, a hangar with a large aerovehicle and three electrocarts, and the camp hospital.

Julia clenched her fists, as to banish the ghosts which were haunting the place and her imagination. Horrible visions of flames and death, heavy like blows in the stomach, and happy memories once deliberately forgotten now returning, like knives in the back.

No visible trace remained of the fire. The grass had grown back rapidly, and the base had been eager to rebuild and bury what had happened, even if in the earth and in more hidden places wounds difficult to heal still remained.

Captain Mayne ignored the hospital and the dorms, heading towards the hangar with slow strides. The place was gray and cold and the pilot, a woman with freckles and copper hair, stared at Julia for a long moment before speaking.

"You want to know what happened the day of the fire, am I right?"

"I know you took part in the evacuation maneuvers in that occasion."

"You have consulted the logs with great care."

"Not so the Commander, I know. You weren't transferred because Rossis didn't notice that you were not covering your usual role that day. I want the details."

"I was with the Landmines Department at the time. But that day I was replacing a navigator who was ill."

"Go on."

"This hangar didn't exist at the time. It was built when the new security procedures were implemented."

"I want to know what happened."

The pilot closed her eyes.

"I don't know how the fire started. I was on the aerovehicle. It was soon clear we would have to evacuate the base, we received the order."

Julia's gray eyes were nailed on the face of her interlocutor.

"At the time we only had one hangar, in the military zone. Medics were running over to take the wounded to the hospital."

A small pause, then the pilot started speaking again, the voice hazy with recalled memories.

"Some doctors boarded the aerovehicles because they were accompanying the wounded. The vehicle I had been assigned to was the last to fly – all the military had been evacuated, and we still had space, at least some."

"But you left the doctors behind."

Captain Mayne's voice was low, icy, and powerful in her deep rage. The pilot's red hair fell over her face as she stared at the floor.

"They were boarding when Rossis called screaming we were departing late. He ordered us to respect the procedure. He said a civilian aerovehicle would come for the non-military personnel of the base. We left them there, positive someone would pick them up. But there was no dedicated aerovehicle, and nobody went. Initially Rossis even declared the base completely evacuated, but he hadn't taken the external personnel into consideration."

Julia Dream

Julia's stare was now piercing the pilot completely, staring at a distant and undefined spot in the void, lost in a battle with tears which were not supposed to come out.

Her voice croaked like nails on a mirror.

"Your deposition has been formally acknowledged."

XI

Cleo was smiling, her face lit by a joy deeply connected to a profound affection.

"So, how are you?"

Julia sniffed.

"I'm fine, the feeling I can't fully breathe is a nuisance, but doctors say it's just a cold and nothing serious."

"Enough to earn you two days of rest, though."

Captain Mayne clumsily wiped her teary eyes with her fingers.

"They say I'll be well soon and that this kind of infection was very common before the Cataclysm..."

Cleo giggled, shaking her curls.

"You are something... all good in the front lines, you return from an inspection and you feel ill..."

A pause, then her tone dropped a couple of octaves.

"By the way, are you going to tell me what you found out? You won't be able to elude my questions forever."

Julia made an even unhappier face, if possible, compared to her cold-caused teary-eyed look, but her sister pressed on, implacable.

"What did you find?"

"The security procedures were a disaster, and have been changed. The commander inexperienced and shallow."

"Is he still in his place?"

"Yes."

"What did you write in your report?"

Julia pulls out of her pocket a copy of a brief document, written in a slow, tired writing as if every letter had cost a superhuman effort. At the foot of the paper, the Imperial Moon.

Despite a generalized poor performance in terms of protocol and discipline, we favorably welcome the changes made in the field of security and safety procedures.

Commander Rossis is CURRENTLY capable of performing in his role.

"Congratulations, a masterpiece in diplomacy."

"Cleo…"

"No, I'm serious. CURRENTLY… Insinuating on the future with a hint at the past. You were right. This was the only victory you could achieve."

"I'm sorry Cleo, I…"

"It's not your fault. They forced you to a choice. Them or the Empire. The past or the future. You chose the future, how could I blame you?"

Julia found herself whispering.

"I chose the future for both of us."

Cleo finally smiled at her, albeit a sad smile.

"I know."

෯

Captain Mayne was lying in bed, awake, eyes wide open on the darkness of the room. She felt her sister entering the room, despite her pace was soft and her back to the door. She didn't move.

"Julia?"

Cleo kept on whispering, ignoring the silence.

"I'm sorry I was harsh earlier on. You risk so much... and that was ungrateful of me."

Julia turned around to look at her, softened, and shook her head.

"You were right though. I have betrayed the memory of our parents, giving up on retribution out of convenience."

"You haven't given up entirely, though. Your choice of words with 'currently' will not go unnoticed."

"Good."

"For a moment I almost feared you had forgiven him."

"Never."

Cleo studied her for a moment, struck by the intensity of the statement. Julia continued.

"I found out I have forgiven Marcus, for his good intentions. But I will never be able to forgive the shallowness, arrogance and sad little slyness of Rossis."

"I'm sorry. I should never have vented my frustration on you. They framed you in this horrible thing, and who knows what they wanted to prove or accomplish."

Julia twisted her mouth.

"Their power."

Once again the unexpected, unlikely sound of the videophone, ignored at its first ring - two heads turning towards the object, incredulity mixed with suspicion on their faces.

Captain Mayne pulls herself together and answers, anticipating with a dry gesture of her hand the automatic acceptance of the urgent call.

"Captain Mayne?"

The unknown figure of a woman dressed in Imperial white appeared on the screen. Julia saluted mechanically, only the briefest crease on her forehead betraying concentration and surprise.

"Captain, I am Counselor Alpha Genos. I had a chance to speak with Secretary Marcus about you and your career. I would like to discuss this with you in person. Say, in an hour at my residence? I will send you the coordinates."

Julia barely sketched a bow of approval, followed by Cleo's anxious stare.

"Be careful – Counselors are the eyes, ears and hands of the Emperor."

Julia nodded, opened her mouth to answer but was interrupted again by a second ring before she could speak a word.

"Julia?"

Marcus's face had erupted on screen, his regular features somehow frozen in a bittersweet expression, between happiness and anguish.

"Secretary, is there a problem?"

He smiled.

"No, if not for the fact that I have been sent to the sidelines again for the assignment of your next task. I believe you will no longer be under the jurisdiction of my department fairly soon."

"They are transferring me?"

"They are promoting you. In a specific sector of which I know nothing. I figure Alpha Genos will give you the details."

Captain Mayne suddenly found herself at loss of words at the perspective of losing a friend.

"Secretary, I..."

Marcus smiled at her once again.

"Don't worry, we will still be able to see each other. But I won't be able to help where they will be sending you."

"Thank you, Marcus."

The Secretary answered with an unexpected gesture – he winked.

"Go, listen to what they have to tell you... and be careful."

❧

The house of Counselor Genos was equal to Marcus' villa in size and magnificence, yet bore a completely different style. The Secretary's house welcomed guests with the warm colors of wood and elegant carpets, while the rooms of House Genos were rigorously white, translucent where possible, furniture in darkened iron or black wood.

"Welcome, Champion of the Empire."

Gaze fixed on Julia, the host was waiting for her sitting nestled in a deep armchair in a small reception room. She pointed at a free seat with an elegant and commanding gesture of her hand.

"Do not be surprised by the title. We have been following your career since the beginning, and even if your Advanced Corps training grades were not excellent, your results are considerable."

Julia acknowledged the blow in silence, sitting on an armchair and crossing her ankles, her face blank.

"Gathering data for the Department of Knowledge was satisfactory, but the Council has fully appreciated that your recent military successes are exceptional."

Captain Mayne offered the Counselor a courteous smile, just to repay the lie. That was when something extremely light brushed against Julia's leg, who lowered her eyes for a second to observe the animal that was rubbing its head against her boot. She peered in the unfathomable green

215

eyes of the creature with a mixed sense of fascination and suspicion.

"That is Khoral, my cat. It's a pet. I can get you one, if you like."

The shift to an informal tone was not lost to the Captain.

"I fear that I would not be able to take care of him."

Genos smiled, a flash of teeth and shrewd eyes.

"I see you are also a responsible person. The Council really was incredibly well-disposed on your promotion."

Julia relaxed, returning the smile and accepting the game. The small talk was over. The Counselor went on, speaking slowly, articulating very precisely syllables and words.

"You have been chosen to be part of an extremely special corps, under the direct control of the Emperor."

Julia controlled the reactions of surprise of her body, but not of her pupils, which widened ever so slightly. Genos was still speaking, savoring the sound of her own voice.

"It's an honor we offer to very few."

The answer was icy.

"What are we talking about?"

"To become a fully recognized BMU, Captain Mayne. A special BioMec unit."

Heart slows down, time pauses for a moment on the last C uttered by Genos, accelerates again suddenly with the inclination of the Counselor's head as she waits for an answer, without suppressing entirely a satisfied smile from her face.

"What do you mean? I know nothing about cybernetic medicine."

"I mean that you are a living weapon, Captain. Every portion of your personality has been forged in an aptitude to war. And now you will be able to become the perfect weapon."

Julia stared at her, puzzled.

"I don't have all the technical details, but I know we can implant magnetic shields with neural activation, synthetic adrenaline fountains, structural enhancement to ligaments and muscles. What takes some time is the titanium skeleton."

Counselor Genos was by now absorbed by the martial power she was evoking, staring dreamily in space more than looking at her interlocutor, who was now shamelessly gaping at her.

Her voice interrupted the soliloquy.

"You would make a machine out of me?"

Alpha Genos jumped, suddenly shocked.

"Oh no, no. Machines are stupid. We can use synaptic accelerators, but we won't touch the brain itself. We wouldn't choose our best personalities if it were so."

Julia was staring at the floor, he hands squeezed between her knees. The Counselor closed her speech with a falsely light tone.

"And there is another thing. The repairing nanomachines prevent the aging process."

The Captain slowly looked up.

"How much time does the surgery take?"

"Three months, to awaken complete with everything I mentioned."

৵

"And you accepted?"

"Since when does the Empire accept a no as an answer? I would have paid dearly the price of a refusal."

Cleo placed her elbows on the desk, shoving away the books she was studying and taking her head in her hands.

218

Julia walked slowly towards her, delicately placing a hand on her shoulder.

"I'll be fine. I'm just sorry to leave you for three months."

"I will survive. Perhaps I prefer knowing you are undergoing surgery than going to war. But the three months will be harsh..."

Captain Mayne shrugged.

"This should be less stressful than many other missions."

"When are you leaving?"

"In two days' time."

"Dreas told me he would like to say goodbye to you, shall I call him?"

"Really?"

Julia could not hide a sudden surprise, remembering his evasive eyes and his rush to leave the house soon after her arrival, during their first and last encounter. Dreas was Julia's age and as a planner his job was to take care of maintenance and development of the Study Center. Captain Mayne's diagnosis was that due to her position in the Advanced Corps and her strong bond with Cleo, Dreas feared her.

"Yes, he said he doesn't mind hanging around with the practical side of the family as well."

Cleo's tone was neutral, but something in her eyes revealed how hurt she had been by the statement.

Julia darkened.

"Does Dreas believe that studying is too theoretical to be worthy of consideration?"

Hearing the steel in her sister's voice seemed to shake Cleo, as if she had spoken without thinking too much about what she was saying.

"Oh no, he never said that...!"

"Good."

Captain Mayne acknowledged the partial sincerity of the answer, lowered her tone of voice and exhibited a predatory smile.

"I'll be glad to see him. We can meet him wherever you prefer."

XII

"Very well, I'm about to begin anesthesia. You are not expected to dream, so all this will seem like a moment to you. The surgery is absolutely safe. Just nod if you are ready. See you in three months."

Lying on the surgery table of the Military Medical Center of Province U, Captain Mayne was staring at the white, brilliant ceiling.

The doctor that was speaking to her, doctor En, had been introduced as the scientific director of the project concerning BioMec units. After a week of tests and exams, the operation had been programmed in detail, and Julia had been informed of the decisions in the same reassuring tone he was now using.

Despite her training and preparation, Captain Mayne had to recognize symptoms of fear were probably leaking out. She thought of Cleo, seeing her blonde curls next to Dreas' frowning face, and confessed to herself she didn't like her sister's fiancée at all.

"When I wake up I will be immediately operational, right?"

"Yes. You will just need a period of training to fully understand your new potential."

Julia closed her eyes, breathing out.

"Very well. Let's proceed."

༄

She rolls in a disturbed slumber, bits and pieces of awareness behind closed eyelids. She speaks with a thin, childish voice.

"The... a... nes... the..sia..."

In the background, a warm, full, calm voice.

"Don't worry. You are waking up."

Julia opened her eyes slowly, revealing an enormous and dilated pupil, crowned by her gray iris. She managed to fix her vision for little less than a second, before having to close her eyes again due to heavy eyelids.

Her retina held the image of a white, tall, laminated and shadowy ceiling. No blinding lights, only a pleasant degree of shadows, apt to favor the reconstruction of coherent thoughts. She slightly turned her head on the pillow.

Doctor En's melodious voice resonated in the room.

"Get up when you feel like it. You will find some clothes on the chair, we will be waiting for you outside."

More clear-headed by the minute, Julia raised an eyebrow in hearing the plural form, yet despite the strong feeling of heaviness in her eyelids which was forcing her to keep her eyes closed, she was not tired. She actually realized she wanted to get up as soon as possible.

She began to acquire awareness of her body, naked under a light cover that was tickling the nape of her neck. With her fingertips she traced the cloth from the sternum to the collarbone, admiring its suppleness. And while she was rolling around trying to find the strength to get up, her drowsy mind was absorbed by a childhood memory.

10... 9... 8... 7... 6... Her self-imposed and not always respected countdown to get out of bed after the alarm clock, the kind hand of her mother shaking her shoulder... Captain Mayne suddenly sat upright, completely awake, and no longer inclined to reminisce. Her loose - and now long - hair fell over her shoulders and at the side of her face. She was indeed naked, lying on a mattress placed on top of a wider metallic surgery table.

She pulled her legs out of the sheet, grasping the edge of the bed – and only when her fingers left a conspicuous dent on the shiny surface of the ledge did she remember the aim of the surgery and the potential of her new body.

Gingerly, expecting the worse, she approached the mirror placed next to the chair where some clothes had been piled. She stared at the reflected image for several seconds, surprised. Her skin, already light, was now porcelain due to the absence of the sun – but Julia was observing in a trance the polished glow of her complexion, the full efficiency of the long and springing muscles which were revealed by every single movement.

Any modification to her physiology did not show to any superficial analysis, even though her lunar beauty was somewhat disquieting, especially after donning the completely black uniform of the BMUs.

The golden light of the evening filtered through the wide entrance of the lab. With a last look to the mirror behind her, BioMec unit Mayne headed for the exit and her new life.

∽

En was standing in the hall of the laboratory, leaning on the white counter of the reception and amiably talking with his interlocutor, who was also wearing the uniform of the BioMec Units.

"So you don't think we will have to check the injectors? Excellent."

The doctor was nodding, taken in by the conversation. Unseen for the moment, Julia paused to study the profile of the two men.

The doctor was a mature man, probably older than Marcus. His gray and longish hair was obviously well groomed and shiny, catching the sunlight. The face of the other man was hidden, and she could only see raven-black hair.

The stranger noticed her first, turning his head in her direction and meeting her stare. Gray inquisitive eyes met a young and open face that looked strangely familiar.

En followed his interlocutor's gaze, welcoming Julia and thus interrupting her attempt to explain the familiarity of that face.

"Welcome, F17."

She tilted her head slightly.

"F17 is your new name. There is no reason to reveal your former identity."

Julia Dream

The doctor paused for a moment, acknowledging and deciding to ignore the fleeting emotions that flashed in her eyes. He indicated the man at his side.

"This is X39. He will help you adapt to the structural changes of your body and will be your partner from now on."

Still feeling slightly dazed, Julia addressed a shy smile in his direction.

"Nice to meet you, X39. I'm afraid I will need your help. I didn't mean to, but I made a dent in the bed as I got up."

The man looked at the doctor, who smiled smugly.

"She is indeed as strong as you predicted."

He then turned to answer her.

"I apologize. I will do what I can, since our enhancements are not precisely identical. Due to previous training and acquired skills, I was designed for scouting, while you are optimized for combat."

"I understand."

Julia had nodded, but concern had become apparent in her expression. X39 smiled at her reassuringly.

"Don't worry. We have more things in common than differences, and I have been instructed on this."

En studied them for a moment, arms crossed, nodding to himself.

"Very well. I will leave you with X39, then. Enjoy your training."

❧

Julia was still studying the surroundings with narrowed eyes, trying to remember where she could have already seen X39's face, his deep dark eyes, the contrast between his pale skin and his black hair. She snapped back to attention when she realized he was talking to her.

"How are you? You got up quite early."

"I'm fine. Just a little confused. What do I have to learn, exactly?"

He looked at her with utter seriousness.

"Your new limits, most of all. And how to activate specific processes."

"What kind of processes?"

"How to generate magnetic shields. Voluntary adrenaline injection..."

"I suppose they didn't just mount a switch on me, then."

X39 smiled at her sarcastic comment, shaking his head.

"No, nothing quite so brutal. There is nothing mechanical in our new bodies, it is still our will guiding them."

She gave him a hard look.

"Are you sure? No hidden control chip?"

"I'm reasonably sure. A similar chip would interfere with the other systems. This is why the Empire tests very thoroughly the loyalty of those who enter this specific program."

As he uttered these words, a dark cloud seemed to fall on his handsome face, forcing him to lower his eyes – Julia decided in that moment she could trust him.

She smiled, speaking lightly to release the tension.

"Very well, I can't wait to learn. Where do we start?"

X39 was looking at her thoughtfully.

"Let's start with the shields. I don't have them so I won't be able to help you too much. You will have to find the mental activation mechanism on your own, before a subconscious projection method kicks in."

He paused for a moment.

"It's good that you feel ready to begin so early. But not here. Follow me, there is dedicated place for this."

⟡

A low and round building, whose interior looked somewhat like a hybrid between a gym and a conference room. The mirrors on the walls could be darkened and made opaque, regulating the lights in the room, while in front of the pedestal with the environmental controls loomed a huge ergonomic armchair, big enough to seat an adult sitting cross-legged.

X39 gestured Julia to sit.

"The meditation armchair is all for you. It should be easier to work on the activation impulse from a relaxed position."

She complied, uncertain between curiosity and concern – he sat down on the floor in front of her, looking at her frankly in the eyes.

"Know that I can provide the theory, but you will have to do most of the work. It will become very simple once you find the mechanism."

He paused to reassure her, interpreting her concentrated expression.

"Don't hesitate to interrupt me if you have any question or if I am not clear."

"All right, thank you. I'm listening."

"Ok, so: the nanomachines introduced in our organism interface with our central nervous system. Our brain is totally in control of their activity."

"All right."

"Yours can polarize to direct and strengthen your magnetic field, up to creating a shield that can stop projectiles and bullets."

"Mmh."

X39 smiled, anticipating the question.

"I don't have shields because I don't have sufficient combat training, especially if compared to yours. My education was mainly historical and political. I was mostly enhanced in terms of calculating power."

Julia nodded, thinking.

"I understand."

"Now, the only thing you are missing to generate a shield is to know how to give an order to the nanomachines."

"I really don't know where to start..."

For once, Julia was completely unable to hide the tone of discomfort in her voice, but X39 didn't seem to mind.

"Don't worry. One way, which takes time but is still efficient, is to wait and try to cause a subconscious activation. At that point you can subsequently use the mental image of your first experience as a form of command. There are other ways, though."

"Suggestions?"

"Personally when I need synthetic adrenalin, I think of a specific emotion. I realize this is easier though, compared to the shields, since it's an enhancement of a natural phenomenon."

"What if I started from there, since it is simpler?"

X39 shook his head doubtfully.

"I would advise against it. Before being able to fully control the mechanism you could overdose. The shields are harder but safer."

Julia nodded, shifting on the armchair.

"I understand. I'll see what I can do."

∞

Two days later, Julia was still fighting against an enemy she had never encountered before – sheer frustration. Although fully aware of the limits of her formal education and saddened by the interruption in her studies, she had never felt stupid – yet now she was seriously doubting her judgment.

X39 was seemingly unconcerned by her difficulties in finding the key to activating the shields; rather, he appeared upset by the effect this perceived failure was having on her morale.

Over the last two nights Julia had not slept much, pondering on which new techniques she could try to stimulate the inner workings of her brain. Cleo had suggested concentrating on an idea of protection, X39 on a memory that made her feel safe – to no avail. When consulted, doctor En had stated without further details that induced hypnotic techniques were useless with a personality like F17. In simple terms, she was alone in having to find a solution.

She let herself slide from the meditation armchair to the floor, kneeling. She felt the palm of her hands on her knees and the vibration of footsteps behind her.

"F17, you need a break."

Since she was tired, she slightly jumped when she heard herself being addressed with the acronym that constituted her new name. She smiled at X39 without joy. "I won't have peace until I don't understand how to control my body."

"You do control your body. You only have to achieve awareness. You didn't build your fighter's reflexes in a day."

Julia bowed her head slightly, weighing his words. She could feel through her hands the tense muscles of her legs, the straight line of her back, the opening of the shoulder blades and the nervous stiffness of her neck.

She nodded to X39.

"All right, I'll take a break. Can I exercise?"

He opened his arms to indicate the gym.

"Of course."

She walks to the center of the room, expressing growing confidence with each step. She starts her form calmly, savors the repercussion and the sound of the wind at every attack, the synergy of the muscles performing complex movements.

She accelerates. The heartbeat quickens but the breathing rhythm does not break, the air itself seems to flow with the sequence of blows; F17 jumps and seems to fly in the air with the energy of the leap, remains for a moment in mid-ground as if floating,

lands with a roll, curled up like a ball, flexible as a spring.

And now she follows no form, improvises steps and movements, dodging and hitting and sweeping at invisible adversaries, completely taken in, utterly inebriated by her new body and skills.

Left leg extended in a kick, she pushes her right palm outward – and the air shakes at her commanding look, crumples in the barely visible shape of a convex circle. A shield.

"Excellent!"

Julia stared for a second at her hand and at the shield she had generated, trying to catch her breath, before lowering her arm and turning towards X39. He had leapt up, smiling.

"Excellent! I should have thought about it from the start, that a warrior like you would have found the way in the gesture itself."

"Nobody had described me in these terms before."

He looked at her in the eyes, with his serious face, and she understood he was sincere. There were in his eyes respect and admiration he didn't even try to hide.

"It would be insulting to define you as a simple fighter. I can see by your movements that combat is not simply something you do, but a part of what you are."

Julia felt herself blushing, suddenly confused, suddenly happy, and deeply surprised by herself. She found herself mumbling an answer, looking at her feet.

"I really have no idea of how I raised that shield. Simply, it was consistent with my movements, I tried without thinking too much about it and it worked."

"That's perfect. Now you have a specific mental anchor, you will be able to create a shield whenever you want. Try and you will see."

Julia trembled at this request, but she couldn't refuse the challenge out of fear of failure. She was trained to never hesitate.

She opened her arms outward, with strength, with a very theatrical movement, and from her open hands the magnetic shields pushed out once again, transparent vibrating ovals which hovered in their position until she closed her fists with a precise gesture, slightly lowering her arms.

A vague surprise and an underground satisfaction flashed in her eyes, while X39 smiled at her, looking truly happy.

"See? You master the mechanism now."

Julia smiled back.

"Mind if I take a break? I'm hungry."

"No wonder! You hardly had anything to eat these days, you were concentrating so hard. I want you to be in shape. If it's fine for you, we can leave in a couple of days."

"To go where?"

"To do some lessons in the Forest."

⤳

Deep breaths, but rushed. X39 glimpsed at her from the corner of his eye, seeing her pale face through the rare leaves.

"Are you all right?"

Julia did not turn to look at him, but sighed. She answered slowly, reluctant to show trust.

"I am… in conflict."

She stared at the sky, a deep indigo evening. X39 guessed her thoughts.

"We can camp here. There are no signaled Terrorists in many kilometers."

She flopped down slowly, looking for a root or a rock where she could sit, with a calculated movement that yet betrayed a tension in all sorts of muscles.

"I trust you, but the last time I heard that I was attacked by three of them."

X39 flopped on the floor himself, not offended.

"We'll be ready for anything. We are faster than them."

Julia pulled a face.

"I would prefer not to test that."

"I agree."

He looked at her silently for moment.

"Why do you feel in conflict?"

"I feel the air of the Forest and I feel... free. At home, almost. No one gives you orders here. Maybe everything is not simple, but it's linear."

She breathed in deeply, noticing she had spoken quickly, perhaps a little too quickly.

"But I have bad memories."

X39 nodded, his eyes distant, his face concentrated and his lips drawing the precise arch of melancholy.

"I understand how you feel."

F17 caught the initiative.

"Can I ask you a question?"

He raised an eyebrow, but Julia noticed his temporary vulnerability by the faintest stiffness in his half smile.

"Have we met before? Ever since En introduced us I can't stop thinking your face is familiar."

The breeze plays with their hair. X39 does not even bother to move the mischievous strands out of his eyes, stares at a distant spot and Julia holds her breath meeting his eyes.

His voice squeaks painfully.

"To get here, we all have to face some tests. Mine was in that base."

Julia closed her eyes, as the memory dawned on her.

"Don't worry. It's almost over."

She slowly inched closer to X39, moved. She could feel his hurt, conscious of the potential of the special kind of pain that memories could bring so easily.

"You were kind to me."

He looked at her, unable to express what he was feeling - pain, anger, all dutifully hidden, and gratefulness, yes, gratefulness because she had not forgotten – if not with his eyes.

And Julia, who saw him there for what he was, someone like her, exhibited an unexpected and extraordinary gesture, revolutionary in its simplicity. She brushed his shoulder with her hand, just the slightest touch.

"Thank you. You words were important for me."

X39 looked at her in the eyes, speaking with a warm and intense voice.

"I was given your files to read. If you wish, I will tell you about me."

Julia answered him in a lowered voice, with unusual softness.

"If and when you'll want to."

◈

"I was born 23 years ago out of the whim of my mother, a renowned Pioneer of Research. After my three brothers, conventionally conceived in a laboratory, with me she decided to experiment the so-called natural pregnancy, following her personal theory that this procedure allows the baby to interact from the uterus with the mother's DNA in the amniotic fluid.

I don't have an opinion on this idea, even if I know she considers my – let's call it this way – bizarre career as a direct consequence of the exceptionality of my birth.

My personal interpretation is slightly different. My renowned brothers own a branch of the family industry each – I had to somehow invent a future for myself, having the privilege of being able to choose one.

So my first choice, following my inclination and pleasure, was to study. Not only the rigorous and precise topics which determine and sustain the activity and noble status of my mother and her family, but rather history, geography, social and human interactions and all there is which is contradictory, disputable, and ever evolving. This is how I ended up in the Department of Knowledge.

I was at a crossroads, to choose between a political career or continue with technical and operational missions. In order to be able to keep on cultivating knowledge instead of schemes, I had to embrace a military path. My roles were consultancies in the diplomatic, geographical or historical fields, bouncing between Landmines and Engineering departments.

And then one day they sent me to R3, where you saw me – after that they summoned me, and I became X39. And anyway, even though I should not tell you, my name is John. And no, don't tell me your name now, it is not necessary. If one day you will find it important, you will tell me."

She acknowledged his story with a look of respect, and nodded.

⤴

Julia opened her eyes suddenly, instinctively interrupting sleep, having sensed a presence nearby. John was standing one step away from her, the waning moon just above the green horizon.

He was reaching out with his hand to help her get up, while she forced herself to shake off sleep and sit.

"I would have let you rest, but I complied with your request to call you for the second turn."

Julia smiled and nodded, accepting his hand and rising up.

"You were right, thank you. I feel in perfect shape and can easily stay awake."

"I can see that. You have light sleep."

"Never lower your guard completely..."

John relaxed to sit cross-legged on the floor on the insulating blanket, addressing her a brief salute with a light tone and bright eyes.

"I believe I'll sleep safely with a fighter like you watching over me."

She was standing with her back to him to avoid invading his rest with her looks, but she turned around briefly to smile at him at these words, answering the compliment. She then fixed her gaze on the sky, allowing herself to become absorbed in the sounds of the Forest, arranging them in her mind in a complete picture of the situation.

Only owls and other small animals populated the night. Reassured, she peeked again at John's dark figure, sleeping just out of the cone of light provided by their camp beacon.

She felt rested and surprised. She had slept deeply and easily, after her travel partner had offered to stay on guard first, and this was a symptom of trust more than fatigue.

For hours she remained in the same position, observing the slow journey of the moon and the brightening sky, pondering on the meaning of friendship.

X39 had revealed his name and his past without asking for anything in return, and BioMec Unit F17 was now in balance between gratefulness and suspicion, undecided on whether she should consider the revelation as an honor or a trap.

"Nobody does anything for nothing" the Champion of the Empire whispered to herself. And yet an older and buried part of her recognized in the young man sleeping behind her someone like her, forged in the same fire and hammered out of the same metal.

∽

"Come! I want to show you something."

Julia had lingered behind in the bushes, all the muscular groups of her body shaken by an almost imperceptible trembling. She had wanted to test her newly enhanced body, pushing it to search for her limits, using the adrenaline injectors - and now she was experiencing the consequences.

They were crossing uneven and sloping hills that very much resembled mountains, with jutting stratified ledges of stone emerging from conifer forests, while the vegetation became more and more scarce as they kept on climbing.

Forcing her willpower with a push from her aching muscles, Julia accelerated her pace to gain John's side. He had stopped to observe a spot in the underlying valley that had been invisible up to that moment. What she saw surpassed anything she had ever imagined.

The green valleys were drenched in the golden mist of an uncertain afternoon caught in the balance between sun and rain – the air appeared dense, milky with light, and between the bushes and the gorge an even more unfamiliar sight appeared.

The dark coiling spires of a road, clearly built by human hands. Some of the pillars that sustained it, allowing it to twist and turn around the hill until it lost itself in the vegetation and the horizon, had crumbled, and vast cave-ins and chasms showed the erosion of time on the ancient monument.

From their observation point, the road seemed to begin a few meters below them, on the opposite side of the hill they had climbed.

X39 grinned slyly.

"Come!" he repeated.

And he jumped in the void, landing with grace on the road turf exactly below them. She stared at him, fully understanding only now the real strength of their titanium skeleton. She followed him, fearful she would appear incredibly clumsy in comparison, but she was hardly aware of having landed, that she found herself already standing back up like a spring.

She bent down on one knee to place her hand on the concrete, where grass was growing between the cracks.

Her voice was filled with awe.

"This trail... this was made before the Cataclysm."

"Yes, not long before."

The girl looked left and right, considering the width of the lane.

"They must have used huge transportation systems..."

She was silent for a moment, before concluding her thought, whispering.

"Or many of them moved often."

For a second, the bright curiosity lighting up Julia's face painted her as the young girl she was – she was looking at John with an open and blue gaze that begged for an answer.

He smiled and reached out to her to help her up, and she accepted his hand thoughtfully.

"Yes, people did travel often, independently and at will. Many forests are full of these roads, the heritage our past has left us."

"Why did they travel so much?"

"Because they could. Because they liked it. Don't you like to explore and see new places?"

Julia nodded looking distant, as if hit by as sudden thought.

"Yes. Yes, I like too, very much."

They stared at the gray trail together, with the same melancholy in their eyes. She spoke first.

"Do you think we will return to using these roads some day?"

John tightened his lips, shaking his head and ruffling his hair.

"I – I don't know."

He looked at her with a sad smile.

"I would like that."

∽

"Julia! I didn't expect news from you so soon! Are you all right?"

F17 smiled at her sister, enjoying her happy look of surprise.

"I'm fine. We saw some ruins today, from before the Cataclysm. It seems our ancestors travelled a lot, and the Forest has swallowed up whole networks of roads."

Cleo's green eyes widened with curiosity.

"I knew it, but the Urban Design Department never took us outside the walls to see any findings. I have only caught glimpses of them from holographic reproductions."

She stopped, observing her sister, a half smile on her lips.

"Anyway, who were you with? I thought you always moved alone, you don't use a plural very often."

Julia was forced to weigh these words in; she answered after a brief pause.

"I was with my tutor and future partner. He is teaching me a lot."

Cleo smiled slyly, curious but aware of the fact she wasn't going to obtain much more.

"Very well. I'm glad."

F17 quickly returned the smile.

"I was thinking... would you like to come visit me somewhere, when I'm around, eventually? I could try to contact Marcus and..."

Cleo twisted her mouth in an unhappy expression, with a slight frown and a conspicuous shaking of her head.

"They will never allow it. And not only the military, the academics as well."

"Not even motivating the trip with a research on the field?"

"I doubt it. The first green light would have to come from the military anyway, so the academics would feel cheated and side-stepped."

"Mmmh."

Cleo smiled, trying to dissipate her sister's frown.

"You know there is always room for you here."

Julia's face relaxed.

"Thank you – but that's not why I said it. I wish I could show you what I have seen today."

"And I wish I could provide you with some of the calm boredom of my lessons, instead of knowing you are always exposed to a number of dangers."

For a moment the blonde girl stared at the floor, as if surprised by her outburst. She sighed shaking her long curls.

"But these are things we cannot change."

"Not if we don't try."

In a split second, Julia was once again F17, the uncompromising BioMec with the metallic gaze. Cleo looked up to smile at her, but weakly.

❧

The videophone screen had gone off for a couple of seconds when Julia turned around abruptly, suddenly aware of footsteps behind her. John had just returned from a scouting operation and was staring at her with an unfathomable expression that highlighted his mysterious and deep dark eyes.

He sketched a smile.

"You are always on guard. Good."

"It's in my nature, I don't do it on purpose."

"Even better. We have to know how to defend ourselves even from the enemy we don't know or expect."

Julia looked at him intently, curious and surprised by the note of urgency she could feel in the voice of her new friend. However, he mellowed his tone, changing the topic and confusing her further.

"You are very close with your sister, are you?"

F17 nodded.

"We were alone for a long time."

She didn't say anything else, watching him in silence, waiting for an answer that never came. X39 nodded to show he understood, to turn back and start working again on the camp, while she stared at his back for a few seconds, not without a fleeting shadow of disappointment on her face.

XIII

The alarmed note in John's voice cuts through the concert of night noises, drags Julia's conscience from sleep to awareness.

His face is bent on the videophone, his eyes grave, his tone flat.

"Yes, immediately."

F17 waits in the shadow. Tension arches her back and narrows her eyes, the question coming from a bundle of nerves ready to snap.

"What is happening?"

"We have to return immediately."

"Problems?"

"A war just broke out."

∽

Julia had to force herself to keep silent and martial, listening to a familiar story, but one where she ignored the ending. The voice of Counselor Eonid, consort of Alpha

Genos, echoed monotone and almost bored from the speakers of the training center.

"Province Y has challenged the Champion of the Empire from Province J... who lost."

The man conceded himself a pause for an irritated scoff.

"So now Province Y has proclaimed itself independent, and our soldiers loyal to Empire are cut off and surrounded."

The counselor crossed his hands on top of the desk, joining the tips of his index fingers.

"The army is already bombing the province. Your mission is to find our people and get them out."

John nodded, pale and dead serious.

"Understood, Counselor."

Eonid's cold eyes fell on Julia.

"F17, you will provide cover for X39 during travel."

The communication was shut before she could even answer – relaxing her jaw she noticed she had bitten her lip so hard it was bleeding.

∽

Raindrops against the windows of the departing aerovehicle, eyes more lead-colored than the frowning sky.

"Flight time to the border of Province Y is 4 hours and 37 minutes..."

An officer assigned to X39 by the Counselors was completing his report on the mission's logistics, but F17 was not listening. Her eyes followed the arch of a rainbow which graced the sky of a place that had become familiar. The Medical Center and Province U had given her a new life and moments of peace. She doubted she would return there.

"... you will enter the base on the border, jumping from the aerovehicle with the Stealth Wings..."

"No."

With this statement Julia turned around to look at the officer, suggesting for the first time she had actually paid attention.

"B-But this is the tactic laid out by the plan..."

"I don't care. I'm responsible for X39's safety and I can object. Stealth Wings will bring us down too slowly, and are too visible, despite their name. I'm not going to give the enemy a chance to shoot at us while we descend."

"But the aerovehicle will not be able to land, we don't have space in that spot..."

"You will fly low and we'll jump down."

"Jump?"

John joined the conversation to save the officer from an argument with F17.

"It's an unconventional maneuver, but structurally possible. We will do as my partner suggests."

"Yes sir."

The young officer hastily backed away, followed by F17's glacial stare, while John looked at her, puzzled.

"You're in a bad mood. I had never seen you growl so openly."

Julia nodded, knitting her eyebrows and then relaxing them in an attempt to twist her mouth in something that resembled a bitter smile.

"You're right. I am in a terrible mood."

"Julia! Did you manage to get a few days off to come and visit us?"

"I fear not. A war has broken out."

"What do you mean?"

"Secessionists. Again."

"And they're sending you to the front lines, right?"
Silence.

The rainbow was now fading from the sky, removing the distant hills from its embrace.

❧

+04.00h. A dive in the black ink of a night without moon yet brilliant with stars – two moving shadows crossing the sky, meteors of darkness.
Dilated pupils in gray eyes calculate distances, movements and turns – yet the unquestionable curve of a smile animates Julia's lips.
Beyond the difficulty of the task, the weight of X39 attached to her shoulders like a backpack, and the risks of a head-first dive in a war zone, there is the euphoria of flight.
Of the cold wind in her hair, of the feeling of constant acceleration, of the resilience of ionized lungs and reinforced skeleton.

-6, -4, -2 meters to impact – an electromagnetic slide slows the fall, which gracefully ends in a light forward roll, as X39 jumps off in this final phase of the landing. F17 closes the flight with a flash of nostalgia on her still smiling face, and the sinking of her boots in the sands of occupied territory.

◅

Their arrival at the base on the border had been followed by a chorus of surprised looks and relieved smiles – to the eyes of the soldiers of the outpost, flimsily holding up against the treachery of Province P, BioMec warriors had just dropped from the heavens to re-establish the natural order of things. Expectation was painted on every single one of their faces, excited beyond measure by the spectacular free-fall landing.

Julia was happy and grateful she didn't have to bear the burden of the strategic management of the operation. X39's orders for the following day were simple and clear – meet the loyal Imperials they had tracked with their airborne sensors and escort them out of the province.

But under the immense dome of the starry sky, F17 was tossing and turning, unable to sleep.

"X39... John..."

He answered immediately to her whisper, showing he was just as restless.

"I'm here."

"We're here to avoid an escalation of bloodshed, right?"

X39 nodded, barely visible in the starlight.

"Yes. I don't have other orders, at least for the moment."

Julia closed her eyes, relieved. And both lay in silence, avoiding to think of what would happen to Province Y once their mission was over.

≪

The following morning F17 departed from the outpost lightheaded and with black war painting all over her face. X39 himself gave her a surprised stare, as if he were seeing her for the first time. She answered with eyes that were made even more stormy by the cosmetic black.

"Psychological warfare. I'm pretty good at it. Any excuse is good to instill fear in the enemy."

She stressed the word "fear" – F17 was off to war and there was no compromising on her determination.

John silently nodded, as they walked towards the border until they vanished from sight in the reddish sand. Satellite recon showed movement of tanks and electrocarts not far from the spot, but from that distance the sand made it impossible to read the plates which would have qualified the vehicles as belonging to one side or the other – no one was communicating in order to keep their position secret.

X39 was counting the dunes, matching the scenery with the maps he had studied and what he had seen from the aerovehicle. According to his calculations, there was a precise path leading from province Y to the border and then the base, avoiding the steepest and most dangerous slopes.

They were now running on that trail, showing how John's intuition had been correct since their boots were not sinking in the compact sand, allowing them to keep a constant speed. The sun was high in the sky when they finally reached what where looking for – deep tracks left by tanks, heading straight up to a convoy that was shimmering metallically at the end of a valley formed by a range of dunes.

X39 rapidly examined the plates on the vehicles with his electronic binoculars: friends.

F17 spins around abruptly, then the sudden buzz of a column of enemy electrocarts pursuing the convoy. Julia breathes out.

"Go! I'll keep them at bay and try to slow them down!" And then X39 finds himself alone on the crest of the dune, briefly following Julia with wide eyes, before bolting towards the loyalist tanks.

F17 is running zig-zag, intercepting the enemy - and then she jumps in the valley, rolls back up, as bullets bounce off her magnetic shields, shimmering ovals following every single movement. The shields shiver and produce a gong-like sound when hit, but do not falter.

200, 100 steps to get close enough to attack. F17 stops for a moment in front of the enemy line to throw two objects at the advancing tank. Without looking back, she turns on her tracks to run back and meet the friendly transport as it gains distance.

She doesn't turn around as a flash grenade and a fire grenade explode in rapid succession, as she leaps forward to skip slopes.

Legs sink in the sand, while breathing becomes shallow and rattling, the convoy now only a speck on the horizon – she pauses for a moment with her head bowed, the time needed to activate auxiliary adrenaline.

A she sprints forward the distance to her goal diminishes, the enemy now limping behind her – 5, 7, 10, 20 breaths to measure the distance to salvation, and then John's extended hand, pulling her up on the last tank of the line.

The time for a smile – then blackout.

෴

X39 had been able to follow the operation from a distance, leveraging the time provided by F17's sabotage on the enemy lines, his binoculars set on Julia's leaps and strides. While the head of the convoy hurried to the border, the rearguard was lingering to cover F17's retreat, with him screaming on the videophone for airborne support.

Julia Dream

All had gone according to the plans – until he saw Julia's face. Insanely white, even considering the effort, the black war paint smudged by streaks of sweat and with spirited eyes where a dilated pupil was all but hiding the iris. John barely had the time to help her up to the electrocart, when the girl suddenly lost consciousness.

X39 sat down to hold her head up, with his melancholy smile taking the hues of a more immediate concern.

XIV

Dizziness and blurry, fleeting visions of swirling faces and white ceilings. The warm grip of someone holding the inert fingers of her left hand. A barely expressed thought.

"Did they hit me?"

The hand, and the answering voice, is John's.

"No. Relax, you only have to rest."

The world and the environment shrink to an endless feverish shiver, a trembling at the borders of awareness, darkness and broken delirious images.

John's hand, stubbornly squeezing hers, constant guide in the confused whirlwind of disconnected perception.

The echo of distant voices, heavy eyelids which prevent her from watching.

෯

"X39, you're wasting your time. It's a battle she must fight on her own."

"Be careful of what you say, doctor. She can hear us."

"I don't see how you could make this statement, there is nothing indicat-"

"I remember it."

The physician fled from the room with a surprised and guilty stare.

Julia's mind had recorded the conversation without understanding it. Her body had stopped shaking, but was struck now and then by violent muscular cramps – her hair and clothes were damp with cold sweat.

John could do nothing but observe, powerless, these crises and the delirious moments when the high fever had the girl either curling up in tears or screaming in rage against the entire Empire, his expressive eyes fleeting from pain to concern to shame at the feeling that he was perhaps somehow violating the privacy of the partner he was watching over.

48 hours of darkness, then the fever had started to go down.

+52 hours. Julia's hand responds to the grip, and John suddenly opens his eyes, shaking off sleep in a

moment, his gaze lit up by a thousand repressed emotions.

A gray and sober eye highlights the request, formulated in a hoarse voice.

"H2O."

∽

"X39."

Julia was aware enough not to call him with his true name.

She had pulled up from the stretcher with her shoulders, to lean her back and her head against the wall behind her.

Her glazed eyes still shone in her pale face.

She was staring at him with an almost disquieting intensity, as if hoping to gain answers by simply studying his looks.

He moved closer, once again at her side. He had retreated to rest only when she had started to regain consciousness.

Julia graced him with a rare performance and smiled.

"You were with me all the time. I know, I could feel you. Thank you."

John simply squeezed her fingers.

"What happened to me? I wasn't wounded."

X39 closed his eyes.

"Do you want to hear it now?"

Her voice was soft but determined.

"I want to know everything now."

John sighed and bowed his head.

"All BioMec units suffer from a similar fever when they encounter a pathogen for the first time. It's because of the adjustment of the nanomachines to the body's natural defenses."

John looked up, staring at her with liquid eyes.

"Only 7% survives."

Julia closed her eyes, her lips white and tight.

He squeezed her hand tighter.

"But you're not in danger anymore. It won't happen again. That is how it was for me."

She opened her eyes, breathing out.

"I imagined there was a price to pay. How do they choose their candidates for this death sentence?"

"Personalities they can't decipher."

"So sending me to Rossis was a test? I guessed I failed it."

"No. You would have failed had you let the past determine the present. They would have found a way to get rid of you, deeming you unreliable. Had you given the answer they expected to hear, they would probably have reserved you a standard career path."

John's eyes shone suddenly.

"But your answer must have shown personality, a personality they decided to place a bet on despite the consequences you would have to pay, branding you as an interesting hothead that can be a good investment, yet not a great loss."

Julia gave in to a bitter smile at this definition. She observed the young man at her side with tenderness and sadness.

"And what did you do to deserve this?"

"I spoke to you that day, in that base."

It was her turn to lower her eyes and squeeze his hand. She wanted to say something, but he interrupted before she could speak.

"... I wanted to talk to you about this risk you were running, but I couldn't. My orders were not to say anything, and they told me that revealing too much could actually lower your defenses."

Julia shook her head.

"It doesn't matter."

John kept on speaking, his voice distant.

"They experiment, you know... to decrease the mortality rate."

"I don't doubt it. 3 months of surgery are expensive."

At those words he answered with the shadow of an ironic smile, the only possible answer.

"We'll be back to Province I as soon as your condition is stable enough to leave."

Julia tried sitting up straight, flinching in pain at the reaction of her muscles, tight as if she had just been training or on the battlefield. She let herself fall back on the pillow.

"I fear I will need at least 24 hours. What about Province Y?"

X39 answered in his professionally detached voice.

"Mission accomplished. It appears that the Emperor himself has spoken against bombing the area, so the army is currently occupying and cleansing the territory."

ᴥ

"Julia!"

As she spoke through the videophone, the shadows under Cleo's eyes and the unusual ruffled look of her curls were evident.

"Cleo!... I'm fine."

"How did they wound you?"

The entire demeanor of F17 became a shade darker for a moment, piercing the videophone and any possible argumentation.

"We'll talk about this in person. I'm coming home."

෴

F17 tottered on unstable legs up to the small room of the doctor on duty. She paused at the door for a moment, observing the receding hairline of the man sitting behind his desk, filling in reports and files.

A few seconds passed before the doctor finally became aware of her presence, startled by the silent and almost spectral figure standing in front of him. He nervously cleared his voice, pushing up an old pair of glassed on his nose.

"Unit F17, how can I help you?"

"What did you tell my sister?"

The man blanched at her tone. He quickly licked his lips before answering.

"I'm not aware of your familiar situation. I followed the protocol, informing the Ministry of a situation similar to a serious wound. It's the standard we adopt considering the... low percentage of healing in cases like yours."

Julia didn't make any attempt to answer, provoking a hurried and embarrassed reprise.

"Event that has clearly filled everyone with joy..."

"What is going to grant me that I won't get sick again?"

The doctor shook his head, suddenly at ease with a conversation which had finally entered his field of expertise.

"There is no similar risk. The nanomachines have learned how to coordinate the defenses during an infection. We've noted that your standard body temperature has been raised to approximately 37.5 degrees Celsius."

XV

Sunset filled the hall with light, a crimson and orange fire veiled by the dark gray of the clouds. Lit up by this spectacle, the eyes of the girls were pools of bright color, barely shadowed by a pupil reduced to minimum terms.

Julia had turned to the window to avoid a room full of stares.

"Why are they looking at me like that?"

Cleo cocked her head sideways, with a slightly perplexed smile.

"They envy you, can't you see it?"

"Envy what?"

"Well, in their noble eyes, you – and expendable warrior – have what they don't have the courage to risk for: youth, power..."

"If they know this much, they know of the probability of success and the risks! They know I didn't choose this knowingly."

"Why should they care, now that you have gone through the worst and are now here, to be presented at the court of the Emperor?"

Julia looked down. When she started speaking again her voice was little more than a whisper.

"You don't envy me, do you?"

Cleo moved closer to her, smiling sadly.

"Are you joking? No, I don't. I know the price you pay every day. How the bonds holding you tighten, even as your power seemingly increases."

F17 sighed, answering her sister's gesture and words with a grateful look worth more than a thousand words.

That moment, they noticed Marcus was approaching. The Secretary appeared overjoyed.

"Ladies."

He graced them with a small bow, focusing on Cleo.

"It's a pleasure to meet you, at last."

Cleo's face burned a different shade of pink, while she answered with an embarrassment that betrayed all of her surprise in being acknowledged.

"I've heard a lot about you as well, Secretary."

Julia joined the conversation which was reaching an impasse, trying to relax. Yet from how she kept her back arched, her eyes half closed and from the way she kept fidgeting to tie her hair, all her anxiety and nervousness kept floating to the surface.

"What is going to happen today, Marcus?"

He laughed.

"Oh, nothing is going to happen today. This is your debut at court, but was not organized for you. The point is to prove to those who are here today that the Emperor has some who answer to him directly..."

"I don't understand."

Marcus laughed.

"You heard me. You are a BioMec Unit at all effects, and you will take orders directly from the Emperor. I believe he is probably going to want to meet you, after completing all the final medical tests in En's base.

Julia's face was covered by a shadow of doubt.

"Simple tests?"

"Yes, from what I know."

"And who is that?"

The conversation is interrupted by Cleo's obvious awe. They follow her stare up to a pale, almost transparent figure, candid like an albino, which is gliding more than walking, crossing the hall wrapped in an unreal aura, untarnished by the clumsy jogging of Eonid Genos at his side.

Sight sees a man – the mind records something deeply alien.

"Oh, him."

Marcus answered without surprise, yet noting the presence of the bizarre figure.

"That is ambassador Ion. A Jovian."

The Secretary preceded their flabbergasted questions.

"They have incredible mimetic skills. They take a semi-human shape out of courtesy. Potentially it's an extremely dangerous skill, but Jovians have always been completely peaceful and friendly, and the Emperor considers our relationship with them extremely important."

Marcus paused for a moment.

"Thanks to them, we have learned how to travel in other stellar systems."

Cleo and Julia remained silence, paralyzed by the number of questions crowding their minds. In a couple of seconds the world had become an incredibly larger place.

And, before she could completely recover from the cultural shock to further interrogate Marcus, Julia scouted another danger approaching. She walked towards it before the situation had a chance to escalate to uncontrollable levels, leaving Cleo and the Secretary behind.

"Commander Rossis, were you looking for me?"

The Commander's eyes flashed in his broad face.

"Exactly. I see the inspector has been promoted, judging by the change in the uniform."

"I've had this honor."

"And tell me, have you been promoted thanks to a history of insinuations?"

She smiled, drawing from her repertoire of Ministerial courtesy.

"I don't know what you are talking about. Insinuations have never been in my agenda, only facts."

"You know what I mean!"

F17 raised an eyebrow.

"You wrote that I am CURRENTLY fit for the role of Commander."

Julia nodded nonchalantly.

"Yes, I did."

"Insinuating that as I grow older I may not be fit anymore!"

At this, Rossis was struck by a cold stare and an even colder smile.

"On the contrary, I was merely remarking you were not when the fire occurred."

She turned on her heels and returned to Marcus and Cleo, leaving him frozen behind her.

∽

They left the Palace late that evening. Emperor and Empress had not graced them with their presence, merely sending written notice of their regards to the court. After that, the nobles that had gathered had started taking their leave. Julia had remained at Marcus' side, following his instructions on protocol.

"Will you escort me home, F17?"

She smiled at him.

"It will be an honor, Secretary."

They first dropped off Cleo, then climbed the escalators, sleeping mechanical beasts in the silent and dark city.

"I am confused, Marcus."

As always, Marcus remained silent, waiting for her to express what she wanted to say.

"The world is suddenly much bigger."

"Seeing a Jovian has that effect, doesn't it?"

Julia Dream

"I... I realized I had never believed up to this moment the information regarding the Emperor's intergalactic travels."

"And yet they are true, I can assure you."

Julia stopped, leaning against the wall of Marcus's villa, struggling to find the right words.

"It's like I have always lived fighting blindly to procrastinate the end..."

She paused, her face pinched by the effort of expressing a deep feeling.

"... and only now I realized it's not only about procrastination, but choice. I guess I am here now because I chose to let go, but also to insult, Rossis..."

"Do you regret your choice?"

"No. But I never had a choice before that."

She bowed her head.

"I've never been free and it's something I don't know how to handle."

Marcus leaned against the wall next to her, delicately brushing her arm.

"I remember we have an open conversation on freedom of choice. Perhaps it's time to talk about it."

Julia lifted her eyes and Marcus continued.

276

"You've always been free. You always had an alternative. When you didn't see it, it was simply because you had already decided what to do."

He noticed her perplexed eyes.

"Look at you! You don't allow others to write your destiny. Your instinct reacts to anything that is imposed on you, which is why you are such a fearsome fighter."

"What do you mean? I never said no to what was asked of me."

"Oh, but you never chose the easiest way! You reacted to Yrenes sacrificing you, surprising everyone. Despite the lack of earlier military training, you completed your way into the Advanced Corps. You were outstanding against the Terrorists. You didn't fall in the trap of the inspection at OB26. You survived disease and are now a BioMec unit, something completely new and innovative even for the Empire..."

Julia shrugged.

"And then?"

Marcus shook his head, smiling.

"And so, you have a fire burning inside you and a will guiding you, don't you think? Or do you think you are simply lucky?"

F17 blushed.

"I..."

"You're not even 20, and have responsibilities and experiences that would make many people sick. I know. But always remember this is an advantage you have, however heavy to bear it may seem to you."

He smiled at her.

"And remember you are not alone."

Julia gingerly smiled back, her eyes apparently lost in the night, yet directed to the future.

Acknowledgements

I am extremely grateful to all my friends and family (I'm thinking of you, Auntie G. and Nonna) for their precious support as I was writing, and ultimately publishing, Julia Dream.

Special thanks go to my parents, Bianca, and Gabriele P. for being some of my very first readers. You too, Flavia. Giovanna and Emil, I don't think I have enough words to express how important your feedback, enthusiasm and help were to me.
Gabriele C., thank you for the amazing cover, as always. And thank you Brad for constantly believing in me, while pushing me to publish this already.

Finally, thank *you* dear reader.
Ad maiora.